OF LOYALTIES & WRECKAGE

SANCTUARY OF THE LOST BOOK .5

LOU WILHAM & CHRISTIS CHRISTIE

To the lost, the lonely, and the hurting who haven't found their place yet. May you find the family and love you're looking for. Always remember that family comes in all sizes, shapes, and colors, and sometimes the family we make is the best one of all.

Because family means no one gets left behind, left out, or forgotten.

Authors' Note

Please note that this book contains scenes depicting rape, suicidal ideation, eating disorders, and violence. We have done our best to handle these elements in a sensitive way, but if these issues could be considered triggering for you, please take care of yourself.

    - Lou & Christis

Chapter 1
Ander

Helicon, Underworld - 1756

"Another." Ander purred the word seductively. Sprawled naked over the bed in all of his bronzed glory, the young prince opened his lips to receive the juicy green grape from the fingers of his lover. Crunching it between his teeth, Ander smiled at Drusus, and gently brushed blond bangs out of the other young male's eyes in return.

They had spent three days together. Three days of food, wine, and sex; not always in that order. Ander had adored every moment of it. Especially when the alternative was wilting beneath the unfavorable glare of King Laelian while he failed to live up to expectations—continually.

Unbidden, Drusus lifted another grape to Ander's lips. "Are you thirsty? Would you like something else to drink?"

Ander grazed his teeth lightly over Drusus' fingers as he took the grape, taking the time to chew before he responded. "Yes, please."

Drusus rolled out of the bed and strode over to the table, pouring them both a glass of wine. Ander propped himself up, folding one arm beneath his head while his free hand brushed over one of the slender horns protruding proudly from his almost black hair. They were dark and delicate, gracefully curved like a gazelle's. They were his crowning glory, and his most offensive asset. The piece of Ander that set him apart from all other muses.

His eyes followed the firm bottom laid bare before him as he reclined on the downy pillows. Drusus, the youngest son of the royal tailor, was a truly glorious creature. While Ander's skin was eternally bronzed, Drusus was like carved ivory: pale and lovely. There was a delicateness to his grace that Ander found completely compelling and irresistible.

"Hurry back, you beautiful creature you."

"I'm coming." Drusus laughed. When he turned back around, he held two goblets of wine in his hands. Soon he was at Ander's side once more, offering one to him.

"Mm, thank you." Receiving the goblet gratefully, Ander took a healthy gulp. "Is that a new bottle?" He swept his tongue over his teeth before rubbing his lips together. The wine tasted sweeter than it had before.

"No, it's the same." Drusus leaned in to press kisses along his throat.

Ander sighed, tipping his head to the side to give Drusus more of his neck. "It tastes different."

"Perhaps all the fresh grapes are affecting the flavor," Drusus muttered against his pulse, then nipped at the skin just below his ear.

Moaning a little, Ander quickly drank down the last of his wine so that he could toss the goblet carelessly aside and roll Drusus over, trapping him beneath his own thighs. "Let's see how you affect the flavor of the wine." Ander smirked down at him, pinning him to the bed with hands on his chest.

"Take your fill, Your Highness."

"Oh, you know how that title sounds so naughty when we're naked." Ander stooped to press a kiss to Drusus' lips but paused as the lovely vision of the other male swam before his eyes, and his body swayed.

Ander rasped in confusion. He swallowed against the dryness in his throat, and despite his efforts, no words came out.

Beneath him, Drusus suddenly grasped onto his waist and shoved him onto the sheets. Ander was only able to blink at him silently as Drusus scurried from the bed.

"Wait . . . Help," he croaked from between parched lips as the world spun around him.

Instead of responding, Drusus scrambled around the room, grabbing up his clothing.

Pressing fingers into his eyes, Ander attempted—and failed—to sit up on the bed. "Something's wrong—"

"Yes."

"What?" Ander dropped his hands to the bedding beneath him and fought to get a proper look at Drusus, who had quickly dressed himself. Although, even in his current state, Ander could see the cloth of his toga had been very poorly wrapped around him.

"Something *is* wrong. But know this . . . I didn't have a choice, Ander."

Ander's blood chilled as understanding dawned. "Poison," he whispered.

Drusus only nodded.

"Laelian?"

"Yes."

Ander managed to push himself up on the pillows. His heart pounded viciously in his ears as his body fought to combat the poison currently working through his blood.

"And why has my grandfather chosen now?" It had been nearly twenty-five years since King Laelian of Helicon had last attempted to rid Underworld of his bastard grandson. So why now, on the eve of his thirtieth?

Drusus was pacing, ringing his hands before him as he turned abruptly on his heel to head in the opposite direction. "He didn't tell me, only that it needed to happen before your age of maturity celebration."

Ander shut his eyes to try and still the spinning for a moment. "Of course, because then I'm officially crowned my mother's heir." A pitiful laugh slipped from his lips. While Laelian had never attempted to hide his hatred of Ander, he couldn't understand why the hatred went so deep. Or why Ander being a part of the succession line mattered.

As immortal beings, the only way Ander would ever stand a chance of reigning over Helicon was if both his grandfather and mother perished by ill-gotten means. Despite his grandfather's several attempts at ending his life, Ander had no desire to return the favor.

"Why did you agree?" Hurt blossomed inside of Ander's chest, fiercer than the fiery pain caused by the poison. He felt breathless as his chest tightened from the blow.

"He left me no choice . . . I swear it, Ander. I had to." Drusus sounded desperate, like he wanted Ander to understand and make it okay.

He refused. Groaning, Ander twisted his agonized body and grasped at the edge of the bed. With a rough tug, he pulled himself forward, and with great effort, rolled off the bed and onto the floor. Landing with a heavy thud, his head hit the marble floor and his ears rang from the fresh wave of pain.

"What are you doing?!" Drusus cried out.

Muscles shaking and vision still spinning, Ander rose up onto his hands and knees. "I won't . . . just lay here . . . and *die*!" he panted between shallow breaths.

"No! You have to stay here until it's done!" Drusus sprang forward, frantic to stop him.

Ander was not going to make it easy on him, and raised his hand, shooting a blast of power that collided with the other male's chest. It sent Drusus flying across the room and he crashed into the table. As metal dishes and glasses clattered to the floor, shouts sounded from outside Ander's room.

The last thing Ander saw before he passed out was a number of the palace guards rushing into the room.

When he woke, it was to the soft din of his mother speaking to someone whose voice he couldn't place but was familiar.

"Was I foolish in believing he had finally accepted Ander?"

"We all thought he had at least grown accustomed to the notion." The other voice was deep and male. There was a strength and confidence to it that denoted power.

"This is the third time—" Aemiliana's voice broke.

Clothing rustled, and Ander thought perhaps the male had moved to offer his mother a comforting hug.

"I need your help. Please. As his daughter, I am unable to force him to cease, but you . . . You have the ability to hold him accountable. To make him listen. Please, Indra."

Indra? Why was the king of Olympia, overlord of all Underworld, here in his bedroom comforting *his* mother? Ander could no longer keep his eyes closed.

"You have my word, Aemiliana. If anything should

happen to Ander at Laelian's hands, all of Olympia will bear down upon him."

"Thank you. Thank you so much." It was at this moment that the Crown Princess Aemiliana's gaze caught Ander's. She quickly pulled free of King Indra and straightened her dress. "Sweetheart!"

His mother was at his side quickly, fingers tenderly brushing his bangs out of his eyes. Her dark lidded eyes were pinched at the corners with concern as she peered down at him, her brow a little furrowed, the perfect picture of love. It made Ander's heart hurt to see it. No one else could bear to love him but her.

"What happened?" His throat was dry, his tongue sticking to the roof of his mouth.

"You were poisoned. But don't worry, you're going to be okay. And I'm going to make certain this can never happen to you again."

Ander looked down his bed to where King Indra stood, broad-shouldered, tall, blond, and commanding. "Why are you here?"

King Indra flashed him a dark but delighted smile. "I'm here to have some fun." The king of Olympia then nodded at Ander's mother and walked out of the room.

"Mother?" Ander began but was silenced by his mother's hand to his lips.

"Don't concern yourself with that, sweetheart. I am protecting you from my father the best way that I can. He will never make another attempt on your life."

Olympia, Underworld - 1768

"So you see, he hated me because my father was a satyr my mother hooked up with on some drunken night of debauchery with her friends. Or at least that's what the gossips say." Ander's arm was wrapped around the shoulders of a pretty little redhead, who was busy kissing her way along his neck, while a petite forest nymph sat on the floor between his knees, gazing at him with adoration.

"I thought you were a muse?" the nymph asked, sipping some blood orange wine.

The red-headed cyclops lifted her head to stare down at the pixie with her one green eye. "He is a muse—weren't you listening to who his mother is?"

"Ladies . . . ladies, please don't squabble. It's as Nona said, my mother is the Crown Princess of Helicon, the land of the muses. So that is the line I am descended from. But my father is some unknown scoundrel of undetermined lineage." His hand lifted to brush over one of the delicate horns that protruded from his hair at the top of his head and angled back in gloriously elegant arcs. "He's where I got these lovelies from."

The nymph offered her sharp-toothed smile as she peered up at him. "They are wonderful. Though rather long for a satyr."

"It's my magical muse blood," Ander purred. "I'm too fabulous to be ordinary." He reached down to press his finger beneath her chin and, lifting lightly, encouraged her up off the floor and into his lap instead.

"Do you actually think your mother bedded one from the servant race?" the nymph asked.

"Hush, the time for talking has passed."

Their tongues had just begun a slow and sensual dance

when a gruff voice cleared itself above them. Ander ignored it, his hand traveling up the nymph's back, brushing her soft green skin, which was bared to his touch. She murmured in pleasure, encouraging him to continue his exploration.

Around them, several other lovers were already entwined. Dyonisis' wine stores had been plundered thoroughly, and as the night wore on, there was an easy progression into lovemaking. Somewhere in the room a harp was being played, accompanied by the lyrical moans of the lovers.

The throat cleared once more. "Your Highness, I hate to interrupt, but you're being called home."

Grumbling, Ander pulled his lips away from the nymph who'd taken to chewing on the bottom one, drawing a little blood with her sharp teeth, and looked up. He blinked in surprise, finding his mother's most faithful servant before him. "Theandros? What are you doing here?"

"You need to return to Helicon."

"Tell my grandfather I have no desire to return to a land ruled by him." Ander's lips found the nymph's once more. Theandros was a swift and painful reminder that he hadn't seen his mother in over a decade. But not seeing his mother also meant that he hadn't been subjected to Laelian's cold hatred or not-so-silent fury over having his hands tied by King Indra when it came to deciding his own grandson's fate.

"King Laelian is dead," Theandros continued, as if his prince was not being seduced by two willing females before him.

Ander froze and pulled away from the nymph's kisses. "Dead?" Numbness filled his mind and body, sending a chill through him. He had thought such news would bring relief. Instead, it was emptiness that swelled inside his chest, leaving him aching and incomplete.

"Your mother has requested your presence at home for her coronation."

Coronation. His mother would be queen. Ander nodded. "Sorry, ladies, I'm afraid you'll have to find another lover to entertain you tonight."

Both mumbled their discontent, but the nymph did not protest when Ander plucked her from his lap and placed her in the cyclops' lap instead. The two of them picked up where they had left off, Ander already forgotten.

Holding his hand out to Theandros, he had the other male tug him up onto his feet. Smoothing his fingers through his hair, he met the manservant's eyes. "Take me to my mother."

Ander could have easily snapped his fingers and teleported himself from the cliffs of Olympia to the forest valley of Helicon, at the base of its twin mountains. Instead, he allowed Theandros to draw him near—accepting the strong reassurance of his body—and snap both of them there.

The palace hummed with the bustle and activity of servants: florists building gorgeous sculptures from flowers, musicians composing beautiful melodies in every wing, and singers warbling heart-piercing songs in the gardens. A new sovereign had not been crowned in over two thousand years; his mother's ascension to the throne would be a wondrous affair.

"You'll find Her Majesty in her chambers," Theandros supplied.

Taming his hair once more with a swift comb of his fingers, Ander murmured his thanks and sauntered lazily in the direction of his mother's quarters. One would never know that a king had just died. There were no colors of mourning or sorrow displayed anywhere, except for the statue of King Laelian in the courtyard that was currently covered in a black silken cloth.

How long had his grandfather been gone? Was the period of mourning already at an end, or was everyone else as relieved as he should have been to know the tyrant was finally gone?

The white marble halls of the palace glittered with the warmth of the afternoon sunlight and welcomed him back with loving arms. Already there was a different aura to his childhood home. A dark ghost had been exorcized. Gone from the palace, but not from Ander's own soul. He might be dead, but Laelian still hovered there in the recesses of his mind—perhaps forever.

His mother's room had the feeling of a hive of worker bees buzzing around their queen.

Aemiliana stood on a dais in the middle of the room, while a slew of servants surrounded her with an array of items in their hands. Menus, flowers, fabric swatches, plate settings, and bottles of wine. The new queen of Helicon was making quick, assertive decisions as each new option was presented to her. At her feet, her dedicated seamstresses attempted to place the final touches on a beautiful turquoise coronation gown.

All of the bustle came to a swift stop once she spotted him. With a loud clap, she silenced the servants.

"Everyone out. I need time alone with my son." Her eyes did not leave his face as she spoke. However, she held back any true show of emotion until they had all left. When it was just the two of them, Aemiliana stepped down from her pedestal and hurried to him.

With a sigh of relief that shed ten years of loneliness from his soul, Ander melted into his mother's embrace.

"Mother."

"Sweetheart." Her hands were on his cheeks, her lips leaving a soft imprint on his jaw. "It's been too long."

He didn't respond, only tightened his arms around her waist and held her close to him, absorbing her warmth and scent: rosebuds and lilacs. She was a balm to his soul, and Ander took a deep breath before nuzzling his face into her neck.

"Let me look at you," his mother said, and pulled back so that she could peer up into his face, studying him intently.

Ander wanted to squirm beneath her gaze but instead simply lowered his eyes to the floor. "I haven't aged," he grumbled. "You know that stopped when I hit my age of maturity."

His mother tsked. "I'm not looking for age lines. I'm looking to see how deep the sadness within you goes." She shook her head. "You didn't need to stay away so long."

Ander eyed her dryly. While his grandfather may have been forced into leaving him alive because King Indra had threatened war if he did not, that didn't make him any easier to be around.

"Fine," she relented. "You needn't stay away now."

"What happened?" he asked at last, his throat tightening and his eyes burning with the threat of tears.

"A foolish accident. His horse spooked and took him through a bad part of the forest. He didn't see the gully hidden behind several large trees. We found them both at the bottom after a day of searching."

"When?"

"Four weeks ago."

"Why didn't you call for me then?"

"Sweetheart." She breathed the endearment out on a soft sigh. "Would you have come?"

He didn't have an answer for that. "Perhaps?" If only to see for himself that his grandfather was truly gone. That the monster had been silenced and would not return. He blinked away the unshed and, unwanted, tears.

Before his mother could say anything else, there was a knock on the door, and one of her servants stepped inside. "I am sorry to interrupt, Your Majesty, but the king and queen of Olympia are here."

The servant had barely finished speaking before King Indra and his wife Queen Juno pushed past him and into the room.

"Excuse our barging in, but we wanted to see you before the other convoys arrive tomorrow." Indra wore his standard swathe of fabric draped over one half of his body and bound at his waist by a gilded belt. His blond hair hung to his shoulders, and though paler than Ander and Aemiliana, he still bore the kiss of the sun upon his skin.

Queen Juno was darker than her husband in more ways than one. Olive toned skin, dark brown hair, and bottomless brown eyes that hid so many of her intimate thoughts. The queen of Olympia did not give much away.

"Indra, Juno, you are always welcome here." His mother pulled from his hold so that she could cross the room and greet the couple.

Ander's shoulders sagged at the loss of her embrace and her attention, his eyes following her movements across the room. He'd dreamt of this reunion for years. Pictured the hours they would spend catching up. Imagined the feeling of basking in the love and affection of the only person who'd ever supported him unconditionally.

He watched the royals greet each other by clasping hands and kissing cheeks, his jealousy and resentment growing. This was his time.

"Ander! Is that you? Come forward, boy."

He wanted to scowl at the term, but considering what Indra had done for him, he restrained himself. Barely.

"Your Majesty, so lovely to see you." His voice lacked enthusiasm, but at least he had managed the words. Stepping up to the king and queen, he accepted their hands, pressing a kiss to their knuckles.

Juno was smiling subtly, something in her dark eyes saying that she *saw* him and the truth he hid behind his smiles. It unnerved him.

Indra, however, merely clapped him on the shoulder and grinned broadly. "The old fool is dead at last."

"Indra!" Juno gasped, elbowing him in the side, which was rewarded with a satisfactory grunt.

"What?" he growled.

Ander glanced at his mother beside him. Her features were pinched, but other than that, she gave nothing away. Feeling that it was needed, Ander reached out to slip his arm through hers, offering it a little squeeze. Her head tipped up so that she could meet his gaze, and Aemiliana bestowed on him a loving and grateful smile.

"You are correct, Indra, my father is gone. Surprising us all. And tomorrow, I will take the throne of Helicon as its first ruling queen in centuries."

"You'll be the most beautiful queen we've ever had, Mother," Ander said, leaning in to kiss her cheek.

"I agree," cheered King Indra. "And I do think this calls for a celebration. Wine!"

Ander blinked over at him. *The man really does know how to come into a place and just take over.* However, the servants, though not used to the king of Olympia and overlord of Underworld being present, were astute enough to know they should obey his commands as speedily as they would their queen's.

Pitchers of wine and platters of meats were before them in swift order, pleasing King Indra, who took no time in raising a goblet and proclaiming Aemiliana to be the best royal to happen to Helicon in several millennia. Ander could only second this and gulp down his wine quickly.

Everything was easier to handle when alcohol was involved.

"So tell me, Ander, now that your mother is to be queen, will you choose to stay in Helicon?" Queen Juno had moved up to his side while King Indra and Aemiliana fell into a conversation about a new treaty between the two ruling kingdoms.

Ander watched the two royals together. Would he be of any help to his mother if he stayed, or would he only be a hindrance? He knew the answer to that question without having to think it through.

"No," he said simply. "I'll come back to visit more often now that I am actually welcome, but I think it's time I went and explored the Earth realm a little."

"Truly? With the mortals?" Juno seemed surprised.

"Why not?" Ander asked. "You and Indra have both had your fun and games there. After all, how many temples to Zeus and Hera do you each have on Earth?"

She waved him off. "That was so very long ago. There was more joy in it when the mortals still worshiped us. Now, they're far past that. We're nothing but fairytales to them."

"Perhaps. But I've always enjoyed testing out the waters for myself."

"Earth? Did someone say something about Earth?" King Indra, having clearly overheard, extracted himself from his conversation with Aemiliana and moved their way.

Ander's mother frowned behind him.

"Yes," Juno responded. "Our dear Prince Ander has decided to make his way to the earth realm rather than stay here in Underworld."

"Is this true?" His mother was at his side, her hand slipping around his arm.

He could only nod because King Indra was speaking once again before he had a chance to say anything.

"Well, excellent!" he declared. "He's a young man yet. No sense in keeping himself tied down to Helicon when there are far too many people and places to be seen."

"Yes, there are many places to be seen. But he has also been away from home for far too long. There is plenty to be experienced here," Aemiliana said. "You've just returned." This time, her voice was quieter, and meant more for the two of them. "Do you not feel welcome now?"

Ander frowned. "Of course I do . . . But you know how I am." He sighed and moved to wrap his arms tightly around his mother, holding her firmly against his chest. If he stayed, he would only ruin the first year of her reign. He couldn't bear to have that on his conscience. "I'll only drink, throw parties, and overall cause a true and terrible ruckus."

His mother sighed and squeezed him back. "At least promise me you'll visit?"

"Of course, mum. On my honor." He pecked her quickly on the nose, and she nodded in acceptance. "I'll be sure to keep myself close to a portal at all times, so I can come back at a moment's notice."

"Just don't don't cause such a ruckus on Earth that they start to believe in us again," Indra chuckled.

Chapter 2
Mab

English Countryside – October 1839

Mab Duchan had spent years in the dark by the time the men finally came for her. She knew it had been years because she had watched as a drip from the window slowly carved a line into the porous stone of her prison to the floor —wearing it away just like that place wore away at her. How many years, she was no longer sure. She had lost count at around the hundred and fiftieth day and never bothered with figuring it out again.

Besides, it was not as if the passage of days dulled the screaming of those around her.

The light from the outside world burned at her sensitive eyes, making her hiss and scuttle away from the guards who had come to collect her. It would not stop them, and she was too weak to fend them off. Their fingers pinched hard enough to bruise at arms that had long since withered to be nothing more than skin and bones. Maybe they would break the bone on her way to . . . wherever they were taking her, and she could add that to the list of aches and pains that she had acquired from years of cowering alone in the dark.

Bare feet scraped against the hard stone of the courtyard as they dragged her through the cold night, her brown skin so dry and chapped that it almost looked as pale as that of her captors' glowing in the moonlight.

Mab took a breath, squeezing her eyes shut, and tried to force her useless feet to carry her—at least then she would be walking to her death on her own power—but all that served to do was take her mind back, back to memories of rolling green hills, and the mist of the sea on her face. Back to the place where she'd first known love and loss. Back to Ireland. Back . . . *home.*

There was laughter in the halls of Duchan Manor. There had been laughter in the halls for as long as Mab could remember. And even on the gloomiest days, sunshine seemed to filter through the windows like sweet ambrosia, lighting her steps.

Mab looked up from her feet just in time to see Èala come barreling around the corner with a basket full of laundry fresh from outside, but not in enough time to slow the skid of her new leather boots before she tumbled headfirst into the basket, throwing it, herself, and Èala to the stone floors in a rumpled heap.

"Child! What have I told you about running around and not watching where you're going?" Èala asked, her tone sharp and chiding, but when Mab looked up from where she was still half hanging out of the basket, her feet kicking in the air, it looked like Èala was trying desperately not to laugh.

Mab huffed, plucking a stocking from her unruly black curls, and wriggled back to her feet. "Sorry, Èala. Brawley said I cannot play outside, and I am so boooooored."

"Well, go be bored somewhere else." Èala swatted her

bottom with a pillow sham that had escaped the basket. Luckily, Gael had cleaned the floors just the other day, or Èala would make Mab help to rewash everything. "Might I suggest the library?"

"The library?" Mab crossed her arms over her chest, rocking back onto her little feet to eye the old maid. "Why the library?"

"Because it is the farthest place from the bed chambers, and I have got to finish remaking the beds before this evening. Now go on. Off with you." Èala swung the pillow sham at her, making a loud clapping sound like thunder echo off the walls, and Mab yelped, turning tail, and running. "And quit your running! You're going to hurt yourself!"

One of the men carrying her stumbled on the uneven ground, jerking Mab from her memories.

To lift her head was a struggle, the strength long since sapped from her body by poor nutrition and a lack of sunlight, but Mab forced herself to look, to see, to *know* where it was they were taking her. Her vision swam and blurred, the structure at the center of the courtyard out of focus and indistinct in the too bright lights of the torches.

Èala had been the first to die—Mab remembered that now that she was breathing crisp night air instead of the stale stench of unwashed bodies packed into a space without proper facilities or care. She had been the oldest of the Duchan servants, and the only mother Mab had ever known, the one who had given Mab her name. And she had been the first person Mab had lost, but not the last.

"She was there when I was born," Mab had said at a funeral, looking out over the bluff on the edge of her property. There was a neat row of graves there, each one marked with a weathered stone, already growing moss by the time Mab had lost the last of them.

"Grady. You weren't much older than me, were you?"
She traced her fingers over the newest headstone, the carving
still fresh enough that it scraped at her fingertips. Grady had
been an old man when he died, his beard so white it looked
like goose down, and his back hunched to the point that she,
and the younger staff, had to carry him from his bed to his
favorite reading chair by the window in the weeks before he'd
passed. He'd been the one to make Mab realize that there was
something wrong with her. Something other about her. She
didn't have an explanation for why she didn't age—didn't die
—with Grady who was only two years her senior, but she did
know that it wasn't normal.

"Where will you go now, Miss?" Kennedy asked. She
was new to the house, all of them were now, green and
unsure of their seemingly ageless mistress. And they all
called her Miss, like she was some proper little lady, the
wealthy daughter of an Irish trader, not family as Èala and
the others had thought of her. Mab hated it.

"I think I'd like to see London." Mab rose from where
she'd been crouched before Grady's marker, brushing her
hands over the bustle of her skirts. "You and the others will
keep the house in order while I'm gone. I'll be sure you're all
taken care of. And your families."

"Of course, Miss."

And that had been it, Mab remembered, breathing in
deeply through her nose to try to suck back the burn of tears
in her throat. That had been the moment she had said
goodbye to the only family and home she had ever known.
The tears cleared her vision, cleaning away whatever
residual grit had been left over from the dirt of her cell, and
thus the wooden structure at the center of the courtyard
came into focus.

A pyre. Mab had never seen one in person, only in

books when she had read about the burnings of witches all those years ago. She wondered, dazed, if that's what they thought she was.

"A witch." Mab only knew she had said the word aloud because it scraped at her raw, abused throat. It ripped a laugh from her that felt nothing like the one her dear, sweet Edward had loved so much.

Edward. She had not thought of him in months, at least, but as the pyre grew larger, she let herself slip away back to that time. To the beginning of the end.

London was both everything and nothing like what she had read in books, papers, and gossip. It was teeming with life, yes, but it was also a cesspool that often left Mab aching for the clean air of the bluffs. The only bright spot had been Edward. A soft-spoken painter in want of a patroness, and Mab had all the money in the world to shower him in fresh canvas and slick new oils. She'd fallen for him so quickly then, and months into their courtship, she'd convinced herself he was the one. Her soulmate.

"You really didn't have to," Edward said, his head ducked to watch his fingers fiddle with the bristles of the new set of brushes. There was a reverence and care in everything about Edward, not just in how he looked after his tools but also in how he kissed her, and held her hand, so softly, like she might flutter away at any moment and leave him in the gutters.

"You said you needed them." Mab shrugged and lifted her glass to her lips to hide her smile from him. When he looked up at her, she nearly choked on her wine for the adoration that lay in his green gaze. Green, like the sea before a storm, she'd always thought.

"We should get married." Edward sat the brushes on the table with a soft clatter as he fell to his knees on the rough

floor of his little flat. He reached for her hands, calluses scraping against her smooth fingers, and Mab was helpless to say anything but—

"Yes. Yes, we should." And then she laughed, the sound warm and delighted as she bent down to kiss him, not knowing that it would be the last time.

Oh, how that kiss had lingered. For hours—nay, weeks after. Reminding Mab of all that she had had, and all that she had lost in not more than a handful of days. Mab forced her eyes open, forced herself to look as the pyre loomed closer. To watch as they shoved her up over the logs, heedless of her stumbling, weak legs. God, she was so weak.

She had been weak then too, at the trial. Staring into the eyes of the man who she had thought would be her new family. The one who, scant days before, had been looking at her like she was the most important person in the world to him.

"Edward, please," Mab begged, her voice broken with tears, and barely loud enough to be heard over the shouts of the men in the courtroom. Men. That's who would decide her fate. Men. And all the while Edward had just sat there, staring at her as if he had never seen her before in his life. As if he had not painted her a hundred times. "Edward. Please."

Edward shook his head and ducked it to hide his gaze from her. He did not look her in the eye again, but she could not tear herself away from him. Not even as that man's *voice became the only thing she could hear, his words so loud they would still ring in her ears years later. Lord Bartlett, a wealthy older gentleman, who never knew how to accept 'no' as an answer.*

"Slander," he'd claimed.

"Deluded," he'd accused.

"A mad woman," he'd sealed her fate.

"Guilty," the judge said, his gavel slapping hard enough against the wood that it made Edward jump. But even then, he would not look at her. Mab was forced to watch as he rose from his seat and scuttled out of the courtroom like they might drag him away in irons, just as they had her. Like his mere association with her would condemn him.

The tears left quickly cooling trails on Mab's cheeks, the salt clinging to the roughened skin where she'd once gouged at her cheek with her own nails to get the feeling of that *man's* touch off of her. A chuckle tore from her garbled throat as she realized it had likely scarred and she would never see it.

"Quiet, witch!" one of the men growled, shoving her against the pole at the center of the pyre so hard that it made her ears ring. The iron of her chains bit into her skin as they wrapped her arms around the pole, hooking them on something that kept her from moving, even if she tried. Not that trying would do any good, she had learned that early on in her stay at the asylum.

Mab could still hear the noise of those early days. The echoing of her own voice off the walls as she screamed until the bitter metallic taste of blood lingered at the back of her throat.

"Let me out!" she'd cried, her fingers scrambling at the walls until she'd torn her nails from their beds, leaving bloody trails along the stone.

"I was telling the truth!" she pleaded the first night one of them had slipped a bowl of slop through the slat at the bottom of her door.

No one had listened. No one had cared. Eventually, Mab's own screams bled into the ones around her so that even she didn't know what her voice truly sounded like anymore. Time, too, had slipped away from her. Her days calculated in meals and how frequently she needed to use the loo.

Then at some point, not so long ago, the door had opened for the first time in years.

The light flooded the room so much it blinded her—Mab's hands flew up to cover her eyes, unable to see the man as he stumbled into the cell reeking of piss-water ale and power.

He was on top of her before she'd fully understood what was happening. His weight pressing her down into the cold stones of her cell. He'd had her tattered skirts up to her waist by the time her eyes had finally adjusted. In a blind panic, she'd done the only thing she could think of: she'd screamed.

The sound had started as a whimper, barely even loud enough for Mab to hear over the pounding of her heart in her ears. But then he'd ripped her underthings from her, and the sound began to burn, clawing up her raw throat like it was alive. She screamed with everything she had, making the very walls around them seem to shake. Her nails swiped at his face. He stumbled back, blood trickling from his ears, down the side of his neck.

"What are you?!"

All Mab could do was scream again, her wail something broken and wrought with suffering, and the man didn't wait for another answer. He turned on his heel and fled. The door slammed behind him, and Mab was left in the dark and the cold again. Shivering and trying to put herself back together.

That had not been that long ago, Mab realized as she looked down at her ripped skirts, her long hair hanging in her eyes—it had gone strangely pale at some point, but she didn't know when. A few days, a week, perhaps. But it had brought memories of Lord Bartlett back just the same.

"This is for what you did to my bloody ears, witch." A

man spat on the ground at her feet, the torch in his hand burning hot and getting ever closer to the kindling. He must have been the one who had come into her cell. Yet, here she was, about to be punished for *his* crimes. For Edward's cowardice. For Lord Bartlett's arrogance.

Bartlett, that bastard, Mab thought, a low chuckle escaping her. Her last memories before she died, she realized with a sense of dark curiosity, would be of the man who had ruined her.

"You cannot marry him," Bartlett said, his tone louder than it needed to be in the late-night quiet of the London city streets. Mab had never thought much about wandering the streets alone at night; a woman should not, she had been told. It was not proper. It was not safe. Mab had never been afraid for her virtue or her life before, having grown up in a manor house in Ireland, largely secluded from the rest of the world.

"I can. And I will." Mab continued on her trek home, heels clicking softly on the cobblestones. It was darker in the part of the city where Edward lived. She likely should have taken a cab home, or stayed with Edward. But she had needed the cool air to calm her racing heart, and the walk to think about all of the things she would need to do to ensure no one would stand in her way of marrying the man she loved.

Bartlett growled, grabbing her wrist, and yanked her back around. The hard soles of her boots slipped on the damp stones, sending her reeling to the ground with a yelp. Her head hit before her back, making her ears ring and her vision blur.

"Get off me!" Mab smacked him as hard as she could, the sound echoing off the walls of the buildings nearby. But it didn't stop him. Nothing would stop him, Mab realized too

late. Not her screams. Not her flailing. Not her nails digging into his skin. And not a soul was coming to help her, either.

At one point Mab thought she heard a group of men walk past, their voices only just loud enough to hear over Bartlett's labored breathing in her ear as he forced himself on her. But if they noticed what was happening, if they heard her screams, they didn't bother to investigate.

Eventually, she stopped screaming, her body going limp against the cobblestones beneath her back. A profound numbness settled all over until at last he was finished.

"Good night, Lady Duchan," Bartlett murmured like a lover might, and leaned over to press a kiss to her cheek just before he rose and set his clothes to rights. He didn't help her up. He didn't try to cover her. He turned on his heel and left her there in the middle of the street, the cold and wet of the London cobblestones seeping into her clothes, and blood staining her skirts.

The flames drew closer—first warming her half-frozen feet, then burning and making the skin bubble—along with the pain of every loss Mab had known, every wrong she'd experienced, every sorrow that still lingered. She was about to die, likely in a matter of moments.

She threw her head back and screamed at the injustice of it all, for there was not much else to do.

Chapter 3
Ander

London, England - August 1839

The sky was crystal clear, the sunshine falling on Estelle's blond curls like warm honey dripping from the comb. Her laughter as it rang out was sweeter than the bird song filtering down from the trees. And though her spinster cousin, Anna, followed just a few steps behind them on their promenade, Ander didn't care. Because Estelle was here with him in Hyde Park, dressed in a light blue gown that only made her rosy cheeks all the prettier. Each time the hem of her broad skirt grazed against the cuff of his trousers, delight rushed through him.

"Come, this way." Smiling tenderly at her, Ander offered her his arm, and only once her delicate fingers rested gently on his forearm did he take her up onto the Rino bridge to look over the Serpentine.

Halting when they reached the middle, he looked back at Anna to make sure she was keeping her distance and then turned to face Estelle. Her chin turned up to him immediately, the loving smile on her lips coming freely and eagerly.

"It's a beautiful day, Ander."

"Not as beautiful as you, my darling." Estelle blushed at his words, and a heady sense of euphoria rushed through him once more.

Just three months ago, Ander had moved into a beautiful townhouse in London, deciding to put down some roots after years of traveling Europe. In short order, Ander worked his way into the ton, getting invited to every important gathering and ball. When he spotted Estelle from across the room at one such event, the sight of her stole his very breath away and no one else mattered from that moment on.

"You shouldn't say such things in public," she whispered, glancing demurely around them.

"Estelle, my Estelle, I do not care who hears. I love you, my sweet angel." He reached for both her hands, cradling them tenderly in his. "Will you be mine for always?"

She gasped, her eyes brightening and her cheeks flushing deeply. "Ander . . . truly?"

"Of course, truly. I love you, my dearest of ladies."

Estelle laughed happily and broke decorum to throw herself into his arms. Ander pulled her against him, cradling her blissfully against his chest. She smelled of sunshine and lavender, filling his senses entirely with bits of warmth and heaven.

Anna gave them a moment before she cleared her throat, and the lovers pulled apart.

"Can I take that as a yes, then?" he asked, eyes crinkling at the corners as he chuckled.

"Yes!"

Not caring about Anna or her throat clearing, Ander

grasped Estelle about the waist and twirled her around, letting the happiness of this moment wash away all the shadows that rested within his soul. When he finally set her back down on her feet, they were both breathless.

"We have to tell my mother!"

Ander nodded. "Let's let her know an announcement must be put in the papers first thing tomorrow morning." Offering her his arm, Ander turned and headed back. Extending his other arm to Anna, he whistled joyfully, walking both ladies back to the awaiting carriage.

The ride back to the Corbyn townhouse was a proud one. Ander had never been happier to share a carriage with anyone in his life as he was to have Estelle seated beside him. This sweet angel was to be his. Had promised herself to him so readily, it took his breath away each time he thought on it.

While his mother would never understand why he had attached himself to a mortal, Ander didn't care. There was a sweet innocence to Estelle that washed him clean of all the filth of his life and left him new and revitalized. In her eyes, he felt like an entirely new being. Something more than he had ever been before. She saw him as much better than he was, which in turn made Ander *want* to be better.

Genvieve Corbyn was waiting for them in the sitting room when they arrived at the lovely stone home. There was a chilled bottle of champagne waiting in preparation. Ander had asked for Genvieve's permission just that morning, and when the happy couple came through the door, there was only joy and celebration to be had by all. While the Corbyns had a name held in high esteem in London, their wealth had been squandered by a foolish husband before his death, and Ander heralded a new day for them.

Ander himself had never been so happy in all his many years.

He spent the evening filled with delight. Smiling at each word spoken to him, doting on Estelle at every chance he had, and finally allowing himself to plan for the future. When at last the evening wore to a close, Mrs. Corbyn had taken herself to bed, and Anna was asleep in a chair near the fire. Her soft snoring added to the crackle from the fireplace that somehow made the silence of the evening more pleasant.

He and Estelle sat in the window seat, close enough that their knees touched, and the innocence of it made it all the more tempting.

"Ander," Estelle began, her voice hushed so as not to wake Anna, "you'll love me forever?"

"Of course." His voice was husky.

"And never leave me?"

"Nothing could pull me away." He reached out to cup her cheek, brushing his thumb gently along her plump lips.

"Will you . . . make love to me tonight?" Her voice was soft but not timid, and there was a heat of longing within her eyes.

Ander's heart stuttered, and his gut clenched at her words. "What?" He was certain he couldn't have heard correctly. Estelle was ever the proper lady, never making a misstep.

"Don't make me ask it again." She flushed this time and looked away.

"Sweetheart." He bit his lip, the hand on her cheek tipping her chin up so that she had to meet his eyes once more. "This is not something you have to do yet. I am willing to wait until our wedding night."

"Ander, please." Her eyes filled with need and longing, and he was helpless against it.

So, rising from his place there in the window, Ander took Estelle's hand and led her through the house and up the stairs to her bedroom. Once in the darkness of her room, with only the moonshine filtering in as light, he began to kiss her. Tenderly, he stripped each layer of her clothing away until she was naked and panting before him.

Laying her down on the bed, he took his time exploring her, uncovering each hidden treasure of her untouched form and ringing gasps and moans from her lips to the delight of his own ears. When they came together at last, Ander was certain she had reached into his heart and made it whole.

Afterwards, as they lay in her bed together, Ander pressed soft kisses to her face and hair, breathing in the scent of her that had become so precious to him.

"I love you, my darling."

"I love you too," she breathed out.

Sighing contentedly, Ander snuggled her in firmly against his chest, happy to just hold her.

"Will you tell me more about your home?" Estelle asked at last.

"What would you like to hear?"

"Anything."

Ander chuckled and kissed her temple. "The kingdom that I hail from is situated at the base of two tall mountains. It's filled with luscious trees and meadows, glorious, rippling brooks, and the constant sweet scent of honeysuckle. My people are a beautiful people, filled with so much life and vitality. Creativity flows from them: painting, pottery, music, singing and dance. Wherever you go, you will find amazing examples of all of it."

"It sounds wonderful." She sighed happily. "It must have been such a delight to grow up there."

"It was . . . something."

"Something?"

"I was different from the others, and not exactly accepted despite coming from an influential family."

"I'm sorry to hear that." She angled her head up to kiss him gently on the lips.

"It's okay," he murmured against her. "It was a long time ago. And I have you now." He felt, rather than saw, her smile at his words.

"Will you take me there once we are married?"

"I will. But—"

"But?"

Ander pulled away, sitting up. "But there is something you must know before you can go." He shifted on the bed so that he could face her, wanting her to see all of him when he did this. "The place I come from is special. My people have abilities beyond just the normal mortal being and live an endless life."

Estelle was looking at him, puzzled. Taking a deep breath, Ander dropped the glamour that hid his horns from the ordinary view of humans and let Estelle see him as he truly was for the first time.

She startled, bolting upward only to withdraw from him and scramble back against the headboard. Drawing the sheets up over herself, she cried out. "What are you?"

Ander flinched but held out his hand. "Don't be frightened. Estelle, I am still me, I am a—"

"Lucifer!"

"What?" Ander froze, blinking. Cold dread seeped into his bones as Estelle's face lost the look of adoration it had worn just moments before and filled with horror and revulsion instead. "Estelle, darling, no. I'm not—"

She batted his outstretched hand away from her before shrinking back farther. "Don't touch me! *Get away from me!*"

He tried to reach for her again, but she moved away from him so quickly that she fell out of the bed, landing with a hard thud against the floor. The fall knocked over her end table and sent an oil lamp crashing to the floor.

"Estelle, are you all right?" He leaped from the bed so that he could rush to her side, wanting to help her up.

"Get away! Get away!" Estelle began sobbing, crawling back across the floor to get away from him. "I've given myself to Satan! Why have you damned me so?"

Ander froze, his heart sinking into his stomach as the air was punched out of him. His skin crawled with shock and regret. "No . . . darling, that's not—that's not what's happened. I'm a muse from Underworld. I'm a magical being, but I'm not—"

"*Get out!*" she screamed and grabbed up the oil lamp, throwing it at him.

Narrowly dodging it, Ander picked up his trousers to pull them on as he heard quick footsteps coming down the hall. Looking at her doorway and then back at Estelle, Ander hesitated for a moment before lifting his hand and snapping his fingers.

Instantly, he was standing in his bedroom in his own townhouse, his trousers clutched between his fingers to keep them up, and his heart shattered into a thousand pieces at his feet.

Screaming, Ander raced to the mirror on the wall and, wrenching it off its hooks, smashed it to the floor. The sound of shattering glass did nothing to soothe the fresh wound torn open inside him, but it stifled the need for violence.

Ander stumbled downstairs, his vision now impaired as tears left warm trails down his cheeks, and made his way to the cart that housed his alcohol. Picking up a full crystal decanter, he did not stop drinking until the darkness took him under.

It was his butler Bromley who nudged him awake the next morning with a gentle hand on his shoulder. Moaning, Ander buried his face further into the crook of the sofa he was sprawled over. "G'way," he muttered.

"Sir, Mrs. Corbyn has sent word."

Ander could only grunt. Was he being called out by a male cousin of Estelle's for dishonoring her daughter? Or perhaps they were sending word a priest would be arriving to drive him back to hell.

"Sir, it seems Miss Estelle is missing, and she is wondering if you know where she might be."

Ander was sitting up in a heartbeat, his head pounding at the sudden movement. "She's missing?" His voice was raspy and hoarse.

"It appears so, sir."

Swallowing against the bile at the back of his throat, Ander stood, noticing then that he was naked. "Fetch me clothes, would you?" His head spun too much to concentrate enough on thinking about what clothes he would need to magic for himself. And what ability he had would need to be saved for more important things.

Bromley had the decency to only nod, his eyes firmly latched onto Ander's forehead. "Right away, sir."

While Bromley was getting him clothing, Ander moved to pick up a letter that Estelle had written him. He'd been reading it at his writing desk and left it there. Seeing her perfectly neat penmanship was a dagger to his heart. All of her sweetly written words of love were now nothing but ashes in his hand, turned to dust by his own actions.

Who had he been to think that he could have happiness such as mortals had?

Clasping the letter tightly, Ander shut his eyes and focused on connecting with the residual essence Estelle had left on the paper. Pushing past the pulsing pain at his temples, he used his magic to reach out to that essence, searching for her.

A wide expanse of water and a riverbank filtered into his mind.

Bromley was back with clothing for him in short order. Once he was dressed in slacks and a shirt, Ander pushed his feet into boots and snapped himself away. There was no time to lose tracking down a taxi or calling for his own carriage.

Appearing on the banks of the River Thames, Ander took a steadying breath, his stomach rolling at the sudden motion. His fingertips moved to his temples, pressing and massaging at the pain that still throbbed there. A firm reminder of his evening and what had landed him with such a headache.

Squinting at the early morning sunlight, Ander scanned the grassy banks, searching for Estelle. Had she come here to escape the memories of their activities and try to settle herself? Surely he would be able to talk reason into her. Make her see that he was not a demon from hell come to steal her soul. That he truly loved her.

Maybe he could erase her memories of last night and start afresh. Hide from her the truth of what he was.

As his eyes scanned the surrounding area, he spotted a lump of blue near the water's edge. The hairs at the back of his neck stood up as he made his way toward it. "Estelle?" Had she fallen asleep while sitting here thinking?

Her dress was soaked and tangled around her ankles, which still floated in the water, bobbing lightly with each subtle shift of the river. Her blond hair was matted to her head and clinging to her pale gray cheeks.

"Estelle?" He whispered her name this time, like someone afraid to awaken another from their slumber.

Ander dropped to his knees beside her, reaching out with gentle hands to roll her fully onto her back. As he did, her head lulled to the side, and empty eyes stared unblinking up at him, a dead leaf stuck to her cheek.

A low keening noise similar to that of an injured animal drifted over the riverbank as Ander pulled Estelle's lifeless body into his arms, the heavy rocks in her dress pockets hitting his knees as he did so. Burying his face in her neck, he rocked back and forth, feeling the dampness of her dress soak into his shirt and the steady trickle of water pooling in his lap.

He had done this.

He had asked for too much. Taken too soon. Expected the best from life when that was never the way the Fates played it for him.

Happiness was meant for those who deserved it, not just anyone who wanted it.

English Countryside - October 1839

Ander couldn't remember where he was beyond it being yet another small village somewhere in the countryside of England. At least, he believed himself to still be in England. He didn't remember snapping himself somewhere else. But then, he couldn't be sure. He also couldn't remember the last time he had been sober.

He did remember an upset mob of mortals chasing him out of a pub. He'd snapped himself away from them, to here. Ander just didn't know where *here* was. Nor did he particularly care.

Dressed only in a pair of trousers and a dressing gown, with what may have once been a lady's bonnet now adorned with extra feathers and pearls sitting atop his head, Ander meandered over a hill.

It was dark, and the bottle in his hand didn't slosh with nearly enough liquid as he made his way toward the ruckus of men shouting and the warm glow of something in the distance. It didn't sound like a party, but he wasn't willing to risk the chance that it was and miss out.

It wasn't a party. At least not the fun kind.

Several men stood around in a semi-circle, facing a pyre that had been set ablaze. Tied to the stake protruding from the pyre was a young woman, screaming in a shrill voice so terrible, he had to wince and press his hands over his ears to keep them from bursting.

Ander didn't know what the woman had done in their eyes to deserve such an agonizing death, but he was certain she wasn't truthfully deserving of it. Risking his left ear—it was his bad side anyway—he peeled his hand away and swept it out in front of him. With a quick burst of magic, the fire went out.

The men shouted, spinning in their semi-circle to wave torches around, searching for the source of the sudden flame dousing.

"What kind of party is this, and why wasn't I invited?" Ander shouted, spreading his arms wide to encompass the scene before him and dropping the glamour hiding his horns.

Climbing down the hill toward them, he watched their dawning horror as they took in his appearance.

"Demon!"

"Devil!"

"Get back, beast!" One man waved his torch at him, trying to frighten him off with the flames.

"Now, that isn't kind." Lifting a hand, Ander gave a lazy wave and sent the man flying through the air to land over the other side of the hill. The other men shouted, scrambling and running into each other.

Chuckling at their fear, he lifted his hands in the air and shouted, "Boogity boo!"

It was enough to send them running back the way he presumed they had come. One tripped and was run over by another before getting back to his feet and stumbling away.

Shaking his head, Ander stepped up to the pyre, only staggering a little over the wood at the base of it as he climbed closer. First he took a swig from his bottle, then he peered up at the girl tied to the wooden stake. "You've got quite the set of vocals on you, banshee. Is that what you did to piss them all off and have them drag you out here in the first place?"

"Banshee?" The question was croaked through a throat raw from screaming, flames, or both.

Ander ignored her. Frowning at her bindings, he drew on his magic to make them disappear.

The girl would have collapsed had he not moved quickly enough to catch her. Unfortunately, in his drunken state, he was not the steadiest on his feet, and together they rolled back down the pyre and into a heap on the ground.

No sooner had he caught his breath then fists and knees were pummeling against him, drawing grunts of pain. Ander rolled away, extracting himself with as much grace as he could muster. When he caught sight of his scotch bottle pouring its contents onto the soil, he cried out in dismay. "Damn it all back to Hades and his pits! You've gone and spilled my booze! The audacity," he slurred.

Sitting up, he glanced at the girl who'd pushed away from him and sat leaning back on her hands, panting.

"What are you?" She stared at him and his horns, but not with fear. A strange mania formed in the depths of her dark eyes.

"Tragically sobering up," was his only response. His eyes fell to her blistered feet, and sighing, he extended his hand over top of the injuries. Muttering a few words, he sent what healing energies he could into them. "I'm not a healer, but that should help those get better. At least enough to stave off infection. You'll still scar, though."

"Are you a devil? A witch?"

Staggering to his feet, Ander swayed a little. His hand came to his head, and he frowned. He'd lost his bonnet.

"Well, I must be off."

"Wait!" She was pulling herself weakly to her feet.

"Mmm . . ." Ander looked at her, thinking about it. "No." Lifting his hand, he snapped himself away.

Chapter 4
Mab

English Countryside – October 1839

Mab's vision was a blurry wash of color that didn't make sense. None of it made sense. She turned slowly to better take in the chaos around her left behind by that—that man. That stranger.

The men who had not yet run into the hills to escape what they considered to be a devil, or been knocked unconscious by their own stupidity, were still running around screaming. Their voices made Mab's ears ring, while every other sound seemed like it was coming from underwater or behind glass. Distant and far away.

Mab rubbed at her eyes and sucked a deep breath in through her nose only to lurch forward and vomit on the ground between her knees. The air was thick with smoke and the smell of charred flesh—*her* charred flesh—Mab choked back the feeling of bile rising up her throat. She needed to leave before those men returned and got it into their heads to finish what they had started.

Her knees were still weak and wobbly from lack of food.

Being locked in a cell for too long would do that, but her feet had been healed by the stranger, and Mab wasn't about to sit around and wait for another chance at freedom that may never come. Tightening what little muscle she had left in her legs, she took one step, and then another, until she had picked her way to one of the men lying unconscious. She stripped his coat and boots from him, then continued the trek to the stables.

Mab worked quickly, ignoring the way her muscles spasmed as she saddled one of the horses, used an overturned bucket to climb onto its back, and nudged it out into the cold night again. A hush had settled over the courtyard, like the calm before a storm, but Mab didn't linger. Once clear of the unconscious men on the ground, she kicked the horse into a gallop toward the surrounding hills, only staying seated by the death grip she had on the reins and sheer desperation.

Tugging on the horse's reins, Mab looked back to make sure that no one was following her. The asylum was small from the top of the hill, like a warped version of the dollhouse Éala had ordered for her when she turned three. All gray stone slabs and an ill-fitting roof. Mab took a breath, swallowing down the fresh air of the countryside, and sent up a silent prayer to whatever gods were listening that she'd never see the inside of a cell again.

She was just about to continue onward when she saw them: giant birds swooping down from the sky toward the asylum, their wings a spectrum of colors she'd never seen flock together before. Only the closer they got to the ground, the less like birds they seemed. They were too large, for one. Mab had never seen birds with a wingspan so wide they could swallow up a man. Leaning backward in the saddle to get a closer look, she gaped when the birds finally landed on booted feet.

"Angels?" The word left her on an exhale.

First a devil, and now angels? Mab shook herself, unable to make sense of what was right in front of her eyes.

Banshee.

The word struck a chord in the back of her mind, ringing true. That stranger would be able to explain this, all of this. Mab turned back in the saddle and kicked the horse into a gallop. She had to find him.

Kent - November 1839

Following the trail of a devil was easier than Mab would have thought. She'd thought surely the stranger who had saved her from the fire would have hidden his horns away or done something to the humans he interacted with to hide the fact that he had them. But no. Mab was able to follow his trail across the countryside of England, from tiny hamlet to small town. He only seemed to stop long enough to spend an evening in a pub or tavern drinking the place dry before he was on his way again—or was chased out with pitchforks and holy water.

It wasn't until she got to Kent that Mab fully understood what the stranger was doing.

"Excuse me," Mab said, brushing an errant curl back from her face. She had managed to steal a pair of boots that fit and clothes that weren't covered in years worth of grime in the last couple of weeks. She thought she looked marginally respectable, all things considered. "I'm trying to find someone."

The bartender looked up, his wrinkled face twisted into a scowl that made him look at least ten times older. His sour expression only turned more annoyed when his eyes traced the line of her hair. She wasn't sure when it had happened, but the once black curls had been washed of their color entirely—not to gray, but white.

"If you're looking for the other one, he stumbled out of here toward the cliffs. Took my best bottle of gin too," the man grunted, then turned back to grab a sopping rag from somewhere behind the bar and started wiping it down.

"What other one?"

"The inanimi with the horns." He didn't look up from where he was cleaning, obviously hoping that if he stopped paying attention to her, she'd go away on her own. "I'd hurry if I was you, sounds like he was fixing to jump."

"Bloody hell." Mab spun on her heel and headed for the door.

She heard the grouchy old codger mutter, "Good riddance," just as the door swung shut behind her. But she didn't have time to waste. She threw herself onto the back of her horse and took off for the cliffs, the wind whipping at her cheeks.

The sea-salt air burned her lungs when she pushed the horse faster, but she didn't stop, not until she saw the horned figure standing along the cliff's edge, silhouetted by the setting sun. Swinging down off the horse some feet back, she made her way carefully over toward the stranger so as not to spook him.

"Hello," Mab called over the sound of the waves crashing below them.

The stranger turned to look at her over his shoulder and frowned. "Oh look, the banshee has returned."

"Yeah. Can I come out there with you?"

He shrugged, turning back to look out over the water. "Sure. Why not? But I'm not sharing my booze."

"That's fine. Looks like you got the cheap swill anyway." Mab moved to stand beside him, closing her eyes and taking in a deep breath. She had forgotten how much she'd loved the sea air. How sweet it could be. How much it could feel like a restorative when nothing else was. "That grouchy old bastard back at the pub said you're planning to throw yourself off the cliffs."

"And what if I am?" He took another long pull from the bottle, the clear liquor making a hollow sloshing sound when it dropped back down by his side.

"I'd say you shouldn't." Mab took a step closer to his side, their shoulders nearly brushing. She could grab him and pull him back if he tried to step over the edge, but she doubted she'd really be able to stop him if he wanted to kill himself, still weak from her time in the asylum.

"Why shouldn't I?"

"There's too much out there to live for still." Mab looked over at him in time to watch his face twist in disgust at the very idea. She sighed, letting her shoulders relax. As long as she could keep him talking, she could convince him to step back from the ledge, she was certain of it. "I'm sure there's got to be something out there that makes you want to stay."

He didn't say anything to that, just took another swig from the bottle and stumbled back a little until he fell onto his backside in the damp grass. Mab settled beside him easily, her eyes still on the sinking sun. It had almost entirely disappeared below the horizon. Soon it would be dark, and the sea wind would turn from refreshing to downright frigid.

"You know what makes me happy?" she asked, picking at a blade of grass from beside her stolen skirts.

He grunted.

She perched the blade of grass between her thumbs and pressed her lips to it, letting out a shrill whistle that made him grumble and try to swat it away from her. Mab laughed softly. "My friend Grady taught me that when we were little. He was my first friend. Thinking about him and the rest of my family . . . They made me happy. You've probably got someone like that."

He was quiet for a long while, taking sips from the bottle until it was only a quarter of the way full as Mab plucked more grass from around them and began to braid the long blades together.

"My mother," he said finally, voice so soft she almost didn't hear it for the wind.

"What's she like?" Mab leaned back onto the heels of her hands so she could look up at the stars newly lighting the sky.

"She's . . ." He let out a breath, passing the bottle over to her so she could take a gulp from it herself. "She's wonderful. She's the best person I know. Kind, and generous. And she loves me, so, so much."

Mab nodded, handing the bottle back. "She wouldn't want you to do this. Would she?"

"No. No she wouldn't."

"Then how about we go back to that pub and see where that old bastard hides the good shite?" Mab asked. She could wait to get her answers from him until after he'd sobered up a little bit. For now, it would be enough to share a drink with someone for the first time in years, to not feel like she was alone in the world.

He laughed, the sound bitter but a little less hollow than a moment ago. "All right."

"I'm Mab, by the way," Mab said, offering her hand to help him up. "Mab Duchan."

"Ander Ruin." He took her hand and let her pull him to his feet and away from the cliff. Mab's shoulders, which up until a moment ago had been tight with anxiety, relaxed.

They headed back to the pub on her horse and settled in two stools at the back end of the sticky bar. The grumpy older man behind the bar refused to give them another bottle, but he filled their glasses near to the brim, then cut them a look that said he was going to charge them double.

"Out of curiosity why were you . . ." Ander broke off making a vague gesture with one flapping hand.

"In an asylum?"

"Yes. That."

"I was—" Mab took another hard swallow from the glass of whiskey, wishing the old man had listened to her and left the damn bottle. "I was taken advantage of by a nobleman, and when I told people, he convinced a judge I had made it all up. That I was insane. So they locked me up."

Ander had gone oddly quiet, his dark gaze fixed on something just over Mab's shoulder. He stayed that way for a long moment, lifting his glass to his lips to take what was left of it in a loud gulp. "What was his name?"

"Bartlett. Lord William Bartlett."

"I see. And where does he live?" Ander tilted his head, his finger circling the lip of his glass.

"Why does that matter?" Mab froze, narrowing her eyes on him.

"Humor me."

She told him the address, the one that she had seen on so many invitations before that night. All of the ones she had ignored in favor of visiting with Edward in his studio. Gods, she'd been so foolish to think a man like that would take rejection lightly.

"Hmmm," Ander hummed, his dark gaze glowing softly.

"What was that?" Mab frowned.

"What was what?"

"Your eyes just glowed."

"Did they?" Ander grinned, snapping his fingers to get the bartender's attention again. "Maybe I just gave Lord Bartlett exactly what he deserved."

"What does that mean?" Mab finished off her drink and slid the glass to the other side of the bar for the bartender to fill.

Ander shrugged, unconcerned. "Leave the bottle."

The old man grunted but did as instructed this time before stepping away from the pair as quickly as he could, muttering about 'demanding Underworlders.'

"I think we make him nervous," Ander said, his smile sharp as he refilled their glasses.

"Well. You do have horns." Mab jerked her chin at the dark antlers that twisted out of his head and curved backward over his neatly coiffed hair. She wasn't sure how it was still so tidy after having been out in the sea breeze, but she didn't ask. "And you aren't exactly making an attempt to hide them."

Ander chuckled low and dark, and took the whole glass in one quick swig, hissing a little at the burn of the liquor. "You probably want to know all about them, don't you?"

"I'm a little more interested in this." Mab held up a bit

of white hair that had come loose from the braid at the back of her head.

"Ah. Yes. That." Ander nodded. "Well, I don't know much, but you must come from siren lineage."

"Siren?"

"Mm-hmm. I think we need more whiskey if we're going to get into all that."

Mab leaned back on her stool, taking in a breath of the pub's stale air. "Is that what you are? A siren?"

"No, darling, I'm a muse." Ander winked and snapped his fingers. A second bottle of whiskey joined the first in front of them on the bar, and if the old man noticed, he didn't say anything.

"You called me a banshee before." Mab took the fresh bottle and refilled their glasses.

"Banshee are spawned by sirens. I don't know how it works exactly, but your mother was probably a siren. That's all I know. They keep that whole"—Ander wriggled his fingers at her—"thing top secret. They stick to their monastery, and most of us from Underworld don't see hide nor hair of them."

"Underworld?"

Ander let out a long breath, leaning over to flop against the bar and nearly dumping the bottles in the process. "Gods, I have so much to teach you, don't I?"

"Looks like."

"Duchan . . ." Ander lifted his head just enough to peer at her over his arm. "What's that mean, exactly?"

Mab grabbed one of the bottles and took a long gulp from it before answering. "Blight."

"Fitting." Ander laughed, and suddenly, it all seemed very funny because Mab was laughing with him.

"Guess so."

Chapter 5
Ander

Paris, France – June 1860

Ander blew a puff of smoke up into the air, watching it slowly disperse into the room at large. He dropped his hand down, letting it dangle off the edge of the chaise, the ash at the tip of the large, brown cigar falling to the wooden floor beneath. A moan was pulled from his lips as Parsifal's mouth latched onto a sensitive area over his hip, getting dangerously close to his—sadly still covered—member.

"Darling," he rasped. "While I appreciate a thorough romp, we haven't all the time in the world. Stop teasing me and get to the main event, won't you?"

The young man, whose once well-styled hair had been thoroughly mussed by Ander's fingers, glanced up from his progression over his flesh and smiled.

"You are so impatient, monsieur. There is always time for a proper pleasuring," he said while slowly unbuttoning Ander's trousers. Parsifal's smooth French accent sent shivers down his spine. There was something about the

French language that he never got enough of, no matter how many times he visited the country.

"Well, who am I to hurry a man along. Take your time." Ander couldn't help smiling, and he lifted the cigar to his lips to take another slow drag, interrupted only by the fresh moan dragged out of him by Persifal's skilled tongue.

The moment of leisurely lovemaking was halted rather abruptly, however, as a sharp gasp echoed off the study walls. Looking toward the door, Ander found Persifal's wife, Trifine, staring at them, horror spilling into her paling features.

"Persifal? What are you—*What is this?!*"

The young man sat up, his eyes wide and desperate as he very clearly sought for a way to explain to his wife just what he was doing cloistered away on a chaise with another man, other than the very obvious.

"My Love!" he cried out, nearly throwing himself off the furniture in the process. "It is not what it looks like!"

"I thought there were other women, but this . . . *But this!*" Her voice went up not only another octave but increased in volume as she shouted. "How dare you! How *dare* you!"

The porcelain vase near the door was the first casualty. Ander was impressed at the ferocity with which she threw it, because Persifal only narrowly missed being caught in the face. Instead, the vase shattered into a hundred little pieces against the wall behind him.

"Trifine!" Persifal raised his hands up to protect his face as he ducked out of the way of the vase. "Let's talk about this!"

"Talk? Talk!" She stepped further into the room, grabbing up a stack of books as she did so and beginning to throw them one at a time at Persifal.

Deciding that he had no desire to be in the midst of this marital dispute, Ander slid off the chaise and began to tuck himself back into his pants. While he had once thought himself eager to tumble into wedded bliss, life had made a very severe point in showing him he was not meant for such a thing. And the more he saw of the unhappiness of other couples, he couldn't help but think life had a point.

"And *you*!"

Ander froze, cigar dangling from his lips, fingers at the buttons of his trousers. "Me?" he squawked.

"You filthy scoundrel! You come here and seduce my husband with your disgraceful, sinful ways!"

"Well now, I'd hardly say filthy—" He was just able to duck the book as it came whizzing by his face. "Hey! Not the face."

Trifine, no longer satisfied with books or vases, rushed to the side of the room where the fireplace was and grabbed the wrought iron poker. Ander's eyes widened.

"I'll take that as my cue to leave. Parsifal, darling, it was a pleasure. Trifine . . . I hope we don't meet again." He bowed a little, one hand holding up his pants as his other clutched onto his cigar.

Trifine did not wish to let him leave unscathed, it seemed, and came at him with the poker, swiping at him furiously, angry tears streaming down her cheeks. He had a moment to feel sorry for her before the poker came at his head and he was forced to bolt or sustain potential brain damage. Running for the door, he heard Trifine following him.

"You ought to die for your crimes!" she shouted, chasing him out into the hall.

"Well, that is a little overzealous." Ander fled toward the main ballroom, using a snap of his fingers to do up his trousers at last, though his shirt and vest still remained open, baring his chest to the world. "It was only a few kisses and some tongue play!" he shouted over his shoulder.

Ander was forced to duck the poker once more, spinning on his heel as he did so and careening into a servant carrying a tray of champagne, then tripping into a large marble statue that nearly took out three guests as it wobbled and fell. With a crash of broken marble, shattering crystal, and the continuous clang of a silver tray spinning on the floor, Ander made his entrance into the grand ballroom.

All eyes were upon him and Trifine, with Persifal following behind, looking aghast at the spectacle.

"Trifine? Dearest? What is the meaning of this?" her father, Lord Toussaint, bellowed from across the room, watching the fiasco.

"Father! This rake was in bed with Persifal!"

There was a round of gasps all around the room, followed by sneers of disgust. Ander could see it in their eyes, that they were more disturbed by the who of it rather than the happening itself. This society on Earth was so backward in their thinking compared to Underworld.

"Wha-what?" Lord Toussaint seemed to take a moment to digest this news, and then he was coming forward. "How dare you defile my home!"

"Defile?" Ander lifted his hands. "I think you're taking this too personally. It's not just *your* home. After all, I've slept with a number of husbands and wives in this room." Spinning slowly on his heel, Ander pointed out the other culprits.

Mortals. They acted so prim and proper. Treating him like a demon for sleeping with their spouses, when each one of them was seeking out their own pleasures far from the arms of their supposed beloved. None of them valued what they had been given. The life and heart of another forever in their hands.

More gasps rang out, and there were a number of shouts from the back. Turning, Ander could see the husband of one of his past lovers—who, unfortunately, bore a sword—pushing his way through the crowd of guests.

"Okay, I think it's time to leave." It was Mab, who'd magically slipped in from wherever she'd been hidden away in the ballroom. Grabbing his arm, she tugged him in the direction of the front door.

"Someone, seize him!" Lord Toussaint shouted, making Ander run all the more quickly toward the door.

"Honestly, can you not keep your trousers on for one night?" Mab hissed, pushing open the front door.

"That is an impossible request. I am far too tempting for that." He didn't need to see the eye roll to know she had performed one.

"Well, I won't have your insatiable appetite be the death of me."

"Death," Ander scoffed. "I hardly thi—" A shot rang out, and both he and Mab ducked, hands lifting over their heads. "Check that, death is definitely an option!"

If they had been in Underworld, Ander would have quickly snapped them away. However, not wishing to bring the wrath of the Sanctum and their ignis down upon him, he did the next best thing. Grabbing Mab's hand, Ander ran with her to the horse-drawn carriage that sat waiting for its owner at the bottom of the estate's steps. Climbing up into the front seat, Ander popped his cigar into his mouth and gathered up the reins.

Once Mab was seated beside him, he slapped the reins

harshly and the carriage took off, carrying them from the courtyard, an array of bullets following them out. Taking a sharp turn out of the gates and onto the street, the carriage wheels tipped up on one side, and Ander felt Mab slide into him.

"Give me those!" she growled, pulling the reins out of his hands.

"I had it!" Mab shot him a glare. "I did."

Behind them, the sounds of shouting and horse hooves echoed off the stone townhouses. Glancing back over his shoulder, Ander could see that they were being pursued. "Faster."

"What?"

"Faster. You need to go faster." With a wave of his hand, Ander sent a rush of energy toward the horses, slapping them on the rear flank. They whinnied in protest and sped up.

"Ander!" Mab shouted, her fingers tightening on the reins as the carriage careened dangerously down the road.

"Sorry, but I don't want my insatiable appetite to get us murdered today either!"

As if the group behind them wished to show how much they *did* want this, another gunshot rang out.

"Faster," Mab reaffirmed.

With his hand resting on the back of the bench, Ander twisted around to watch the mob and was truly impressed with himself at the sight of them all. He hadn't thought he would stir up such a crowd, having only called out a few people for their sexual exploits. But it would seem some had joined in for the mere sport of it.

"I thought the French were lovers, not vengeful lunatics," he muttered, turning back around in time to see that the street they were racing down led straight to the Seine River, and Mab didn't seem intent on slowing down. "Mabbers, my love, I think we need to slow down to make that turn!"

"No, we don't."

"What?" He looked over at her to make certain his friend hadn't lost her mind.

"We don't need to slow down. You need to free the horses, and we need to jump."

Ander waved his hands before him, the spark of his cigar creating a red swirling trail in the night air. "I don't jump. Jumping is a terrible idea. Why would we jump?!"

"Just do it, Ander!"

The river was coming up on them more quickly than he would have liked, and they would soon be without any room to do anything. Letting out a scream of distress, Ander wove a blast of magic over the horses' harnesses, releasing them.

"Now!" Mab shouted just as the carriage front began to dip down.

Still screaming, Ander jumped from his side of the carriage, cushioning their tumble with magic as best he could. The impact was still intense enough to knock the air out of his lungs. Ander rolled down the hill until finally fetching up on some barrels.

Groaning, he lifted his hand into the air, the brown cigar still clasped between his fingers. "I didn't lose it!"

There was only an incoherent grumble from Mab in response. Soon she was at his side, hauling him behind the barrels as the mob of angry Frenchmen stampeded past. Both watched them go by and down to the Seine, where the carriage was disappearing beneath the river's surface.

Still panting, their eyes finally met. Both were

incredibly rumpled, but Ander's magic had protected them enough to prevent any real injuries.

"I think it's time we left France," Mab stated blandly.

"I've always liked Spain . . ."

Chapter 6
Mab

Barcelona, Spain - July 1860

"You know, I don't think I've ever seen one of my kind out in the wild before," a voice said just loudly enough for Mab to hear over the revelry around them.

"One of your kind?" Mab turned to take in the warm brown face of a young woman standing behind her with a glass of sangria held aloft as if she were toasting Mab. "What do you mean one of your kind?"

"A siren." The woman shrugged, seeming unbothered by the suspicion Mab was sure lined her face. "Or a banshee, rather." She nodded to the white curls which Mab had only pulled half back into some semblance of the current fashion—she didn't have it in her to tangle with one of those braided monstrosities most women wore, and Ander had been busy with his own preparations. "Even rarer."

"Rarer?" Mab took another drink from her glass, her attention now fully on the stranger. Over the years since joining Ander on his misadventures around Europe, she'd

63

gotten used to being surrounded by creatures of all types. But this was the first she'd seen of anyone else like her. Ander had told her once that they kept to themselves, sheltered away in a monastery somewhere in Underworld.

The woman tilted her head, one lock of light brown hair —pulled intentionally from the woman's tightly wrapped hairstyle to accentuate her long neck—fell across her cheek. Mab shifted under her gaze, unused to being assessed up close by another person after so many years of living in Ander's shadow. "You weren't born in Sophelia, were you?"

"Where?" Mab blinked.

"Oh. You really don't know anything about what you are?" The woman shook her head, setting her drink on a nearby table before she reached for Mab's hands. "I'm Ronen. Come sit with me, let's talk."

Mab nodded, dazed by the flood of information, and let Ronen led her to one of the small settees that Ander had lining the walls of their parlor. With one glance around the room to find her friend, Mab settled beside the other woman. Ander was on the dance floor, his face pressed scandalously close to the neck of a spritely young woman with long blond hair. At least he was unlikely to get into trouble in their own home. Mab thanked the gods for small mercies.

"Where were you born? Tell me all about you." Ronen hadn't let go of Mab's hands yet. She was squeezing the fingers a little more tightly than might have been polite, but there was an interest and curiosity in her warm brown eyes that Mab couldn't quite ignore.

"First, tell me why banshees are rarer than sirens." Mab shifted to get more comfortable on the hard cushions. She hadn't had nearly enough to drink to want to go through her whole life story with a stranger, but Ronen seemed sweet, and the curiosity in her gaze would likely eat away at Mab before the night was through.

"Because most of us are born in Sophelia and never leave. Sophelia was built to protect us from the trauma that turns a siren into a banshee. Which means . . ." Ronen's words tapered off and her gaze immediately grew sad. "Oh, you poor child. You don't have to tell me how you got this way if you don't want to."

And that sealed it for Mab. She spent the rest of the party telling Ronen everything about her life before she met Ander, and how she had gone from a siren to a banshee. She let the whole story unravel like a spool of thread, waiting for the moment when Ronen would sneer at her in disgust with bated breath. It never came. And by the end of the story, Ronen had taken her hands again, squeezing them so tight Mab could feel her knuckles rubbing against one another.

"You have to come back with me to Sophelia. You need to learn about our people, and everything you're capable of. Please. Please, come back with me."

Mab swallowed roughly around an ache in her throat that was born either of talking too much, emotion, or the guilt of leaving her first friend behind to face the world alone. She looked around again, searching for Ander's long, spindly horns, and found him in a corner with the same blond girl draped over him.

"I have to check with my friend," Mab said by way of answer. She had more than paid her debt to him over the years, but could she leave him? Even if it wasn't permanent? Would he be lonely without her?

Ander's laugh rang out above the muffled chatter of the room, his head thrown back in absolute delight at something the little sprite had just said.

No. He probably wouldn't be lonely without her.

"You should go," Ander said two days later, when all of their guests had cleared out and they were having brunch while on the patio. The sun glinted off the rings on his fingers as he picked up his glass. She didn't know what she'd been expecting him to say. Maybe she'd expected him to ask her to stay, to tell her that he needed her, but no. No, he'd just agreed that she should go.

"What about you? Who will pull you out of trouble next time you—"

"Mabbers, darling," Ander laughed, shaking his head, "I've been looking after myself for over a century now. I don't think a few months without my babysitter will do me any harm."

Mab nodded, taking up her glass to suck down the last of the sangria and refill it before she spoke again.

"I wish you could come with me." The words were small in her mouth, fragile, but they sounded silly to her own ears. She was not a child; she didn't need Ander there to hold her hand while she delved into a world she didn't know or understand. But he'd been there when she'd needed someone the most and had continued to be ever since.

"Wouldn't that be ridiculous. Me? At a monastery?" Ander threw his head back and laughed loud enough that it echoed off the walls of their home. When he was finished, he looked at her with one of his too-bright smiles and said, "Seriously, don't worry about me, Mabbers. I'll be fine. You should go and learn about where you come from. You might not get another chance."

And that was the end of that.

The Sea of Clotho, Underworld - July 1860

How was it that every time Mab Duchan got on a boat, she felt like she was running away from home? First from Ireland, and now from Ander. She'd boarded the boat after following Ronen through a door of a seemingly innocuous café in the mortal realm that led directly into Underworld, then to a dock on the Sea of Clotho. Then onto a ship that would take them to the monastery of Sophelia.

"There it is," Ronen said, her shoulder pressed against Mab's where they leaned against the railing of the ship.

Sophelia was breathtaking. The white stones that made up the fortress were dyed peach by the slowly sinking sun. Waves lapped gently against the walls, making it look like Sophelia had simply risen out of the sea rather than being built.

"Welcome to Sophelia, Sister Mab." Ronen laughed, jostling Mab a little harder. The word *sister* sounded strange to Mab's ears. She'd never been anyone's sister before, and she didn't think it meant the same thing to Ronen that it meant to her. It didn't ring with the same feeling "Mabbers" did when Ander said it. "Are you ready to meet your people?"

"Yes." Mab let the word out on a breath, her hands gripping the railing tight enough that her knuckles ached with the pressure.

There was a small group of women waiting for them

when they docked. Sweeping midnight-blue robes brushed the age-worn wood, and hoods hid the women's faces from the majority of the fading sun.

"Sister Cassia." Ronen stepped forward to dip her head into a low bow before the woman at the front of the contingent. "It is good to see you again."

"And you, Sister Ronen." Cassia pulled her hood back to reveal warm copper skin and brown eyes sparkling with what seemed to Mab like years of wisdom. "I see you have brought with you a friend."

"Oh, yes! This is Mab Duchan." Ronen held her hands out to Mab, gesturing her forward. "She is an Unseen."

"A what?" Mab moved to stand beside Ronen, shifting back on her heels when the eyes of the entire group locked on her, their gazes judging, trying to decide if she fit with them. And Mab couldn't help but feel like she came up lacking.

"It means someone who was born in the mortal realm and has never been home." Ronen fixed Mab with a smile. The word "home" sank like lead into Mab's stomach. *Home.* Was Sophelia home? Were these people home? She shook herself. She was too close to getting answers to let herself be bogged down by semantics.

"Come. Let us show you around." Cassia turned and started back down the dock, not stopping to make sure the others were following behind, and Mab stumbled a little on wobbly legs to keep up. "Sister Danae, while I show our new sister the gardens and the library, why don't you see to preparing a room for her?"

One of the women in the group nodded, and once they were through the gates of Sophelia, Mab was left singularly in the company of Cassia, the others branching off to see to their responsibilities.

"So, uh . . . this place is nice." Mab shifted on her feet, clasping her hands behind her back in hope of hiding how they shook. Her gaze swept the darkened courtyard covered in more plants than Mab thought she'd ever seen in one place before. Fruit dangled from a nearby tree, rustling in the breeze, which strangely did not smell of salt and seawater or even the flowering vegetation of the courtyard. It smelt of . . . *nothing*. Just air. Empty and strange. Unsettling when one was used to the constant onslaught of smells in the mortal world.

"Yes. Nice," Cassia said delicately. "Before we meet with the rest of our people for supper, I must ask if you've had any prophecies while in the mortal realm. We like to get them on record as soon as possible." Cassia turned off the path to lead Mab to a set of midnight-blue double doors with gilded handles.

"Prophecies?" Mab wrinkled her nose, her eyes swiveling back to Cassia.

"Yes. Our kind are well known to be oracles of a fashion. Sirens have visions of all kinds. The future, the past, the present. The rise of kingdoms, the fall of kings. Anything. But with one of *your kind* . . ." The words were said with an emotion Mab couldn't pinpoint. It wasn't fear or revulsion. Maybe it was pity. But she'd only just met Cassia, and it was hard to tell. "They are always of the death of a family member. That is why so many mortal stories call banshees death omens. Your predecessors were women who tried to warn their loved ones that death was coming for them and were punished for it."

"No." Mab swallowed around a knot of unease that had settled into her chest. "No, I haven't had any visions like that."

Cassia turned to look at her, her eyes narrowed as she

assessed something on Mab's face, and Mab shifted under her suspicion. "That is good," Cassia said when she seemed to determine that Mab had been telling the truth. "Then Ronen got to you in time." She pushed the doors open and stepped through, seeming to expect Mab to follow her.

"In time for what?" Mab's head turned, taking in the towering shelves that spanned every wall, seeming to reach up to the sky. Each shelf was divided into smaller nooks, and in those nooks were stacked scroll upon scroll. Rolled tight, and not organized in any way that Mab could discern at a glance.

"In time to stop you from breaking one of our most sacred laws." Cassia continued walking, over to one of the shelves, and pulled a scroll before she made her way to the big table at the center of the room. She nodded for Mab to join her. "One of our core tenets is that we do not interfere in the lives of others"

"So if someone has one of these prophecies, you just. . ."

"Write it down and add it to our records," Cassia said, unfurling the scroll so Mab could see the words flowing across the page. They didn't look like they had been hand-written or typed, and they moved in such a way that reminded her of waves rippling with the tides. She leaned closer to get a better look and swore she could hear a voice echoing from the ink. "Every prophecy brought to us is added to the record and stored away here."

"Stored away?"

"Yes. To keep them from falling into the wrong hands, of course."

"Of course." Mab frowned but bit down on the inside of her cheek.

A bell rang somewhere out in the gardens, and Cassia looked up with a smile, her fingers already working to put the scroll away. "Come, I'll show you to the dining hall. It's supper time."

Mab followed her back out into the courtyard and to another set of double doors that opened onto a large dining hall. The benches were packed with women of all ages and ethnicities. But even from the limited perspective of the door, Mab could only count a handful of white heads. Just a few like her. And while many of the women sat close enough to hold conversations, Mab couldn't see anyone actually talking. Instead, the air was full of only the soft sound of cutlery on dishes. "We do not speak during meals. Come, I will help you find a seat."

"You don't speak during meals?" Mab squeaked, her feet stumbling along behind Cassia again. Her skin prickled with people's eyes on her. No one said a word, but she could feel them assessing her, judging her, looking for some sign that she didn't fit.

"I think you'll find that much of life in Sophelia is very different from what you have known of the mortal world. To engender an environment of peace and tranquility, speaking is kept to necessity alone." Cassia held out a full bowl to Mab. "Why don't we sit with Sister Ronen?"

"Uh . . . yeah. Sure." Mab frowned down at the bowl of rice in her hands and followed Cassia to an empty spot on a bench beside Ronen. She didn't see the point in sitting beside someone she knew when she wouldn't be allowed to talk to them . . .

Ronen gave a little wave, and everyone went back to eating as if none of it had happened. Mab bit the inside of her cheek again to swallow down anything she may have wanted to say.

She did *want* to fit here. She'd just . . . Well, she supposed she'd have to try.

Chapter 7
Ander

Thespies, Greece — August 1860

Ander spent two weeks in Barcelona living his life to the fullest, until the true emptiness of his and Mab's villa really sunk in. The rooms were too silent, the walls too judgmental, and the furniture too cold. His entire home had lost all of its appeal. At first Ander had convinced himself he was simply getting tired of Spain. In truth, the problem was that Mab wasn't there to share any of it with him. The solution for both was still the same.

It was time to leave Spain.

Thespies wasn't exactly an exciting village by human standards. However, it *was* the preferred home of Erotes, who had chosen it out of a sense of fondness for the ancient city it was named after. The Festival of Eros had taken place in Thespiae, and the 'god of love' enjoyed regaling anyone he could corner with the tale of the celebration once thrown in his honor.

It didn't matter that Thespiae didn't even exist anymore. It didn't matter to any of the gods from Olympia that their ancient times of worship had passed. The tales of glory were enough to carry all of them for another millennia or two.

Ander stood in the midst of a wonderfully hedonistic evening as men and women danced and gyrated all over the room. Moans spilled out from every corner and were only overpowered by the tinkling of glasses and the lyre player, who wore nothing but a haphazardly wrapped toga around her waist.

Erotes knew how to live up to his name.

Ander had dressed to fit in with the Underworld party: a gold sarong hung low on his narrow hips, showing off the deep V that ran along his abdomen and pointed toward the hidden prize beneath the golden fabric. Several bands of gold wrapped around his biceps, and at his wrists he bore thick cuffs of matching gold. It felt wonderful to be out of the stuffy, overly modest apparel of the human world and in clothes more befitting his physique.

Catching the eye of a fetching woman who stood near a dark, tempting doorway, Ander smiled slowly. Much like Ander, she wore a swatch of cloth around her hips. Unlike Ander, her chest was covered by a cascade of honey-brown hair—only the cascade of hair. He recognized the offer in her eyes just as easily as he recognized her—he'd know his hostess anywhere. Feeling a smirk tugging at his lips, Ander made his way toward her, a panther stalking his prey.

Atama knew she had his acceptance without needing to ask and, taking his hand, led Ander through the doorway and down into the wine cellar of the villa. Neither spoke as they stripped each other of their sole garments and locked their lips in a battle of wills and pleasure. When all was said and done, Ander lay sprawled over a set of barrels with

Atama collapsed on top of him, his length still buried deep inside her.

"Goddess . . . there is no wonder you captured the hand of the god of sex and love, no other man could hope to live up to you," Ander sighed in sated pleasure.

His nerve-endings tingled, and his muscles were heavy and languid. Atama had made him work for it: all over every inch of the wine cellar, every surface they could reach, in multiple positions. Until the two of them had moaned their throats raw and could no longer hold themselves up.

"Mm, you didn't do too bad yourself." Atama purred her words against his chest, her fingers toying lightly with his nipple.

"Why thank—"

"What year would you like me to bring up, master?"

"I was thinking to unstop the barrel of 1720—Atama?!"

The voices of Erotes and his faithful satyr servant broke the post-coital bliss and had Atama and Ander bolting into an upright position. Which only made both of them moan, as the friction caused Ander to harden again, and the jerk of his hips rubbed against Atama's overstimulated body.

Looking at Erotes, Ander could have sworn his eyes turned blood-red. What he *was* positive of, though, was the gold bow and arrow that had materialized out of nowhere, straight into the god's hands. Without a second thought, Ander shoved the goddess off his lap and flipped backward off the barrels.

"I can explain!" Atama yelped from her heap on the floor.

"I think it's all pretty self-explanatory, Atama!" Ander shushed, waving his hand at her from behind the wine barrel as the first arrow whizzed overhead, sinking into another behind him. "He doesn't need help!"

"No, I do not need help seeing when I am being cuckolded by a serpent of the lowest degree!" Erotes bellowed.

"Excuse me, I take offense to that!" Ander couldn't help popping up to defend himself.

It provided Erotes with the shot he needed, and another arrow narrowly missed him, clanging off one of his horns and making him moan from the vibrations and pain thrumming down into his head.

"I don't care what you say. Nor do I care what Indra says. You will die here tonight, scoundrel prince of Helicon!"

"I kind of like that title," Ander called out, crawling on hands and knees toward a large stack of barrels and ducking behind them.

Peering out through a crack between the barrels, he saw that Erotes was closing in on him, and Amata had decided it was best to stay out of this and flee while she could. Knowing he would get no aid by way of the angry god's wife, Ander did what he had to and sent a blast of power toward the wall of barrels. Perhaps if he could distract Erotes enough, he'd be able to remain here at the party and see where the rest of his night took him.

As the wood tumbled and cracked open, sending wave upon wave of red and white wine spilling out over the floor, Ander fled. Blowing a hole in the ceiling above him, he launched himself up through the opening and into the main level of the villa. Couples broke apart in surprise, staring at the wine-drenched, naked man, his horns glinting in the candlelight.

Below him, Erotes let out a terrifying howl of fury, and Ander smiled weakly at the couple closest to him. "He can't find the wine he wanted."

A rumble began in the depths of the cellar and made its way up through the villa walls. Erotes may be the fabled god of love, but at this moment, Ander was certain he had traded places with Hades and was looking to bring a world of death down upon his head. The floor beneath them began to crack, and a large hand slipped through to swing at Ander's ankle.

Yelping, he lurched out of the way. *Since when did Erotes gain the ability to shift in size?*

"Ander Ruin, I will end you!"

The booming voice echoed inside his chest and left Ander's knees feeling weaker than he'd care to remember.

"I think we can come to a peaceful resolution on this, surely. How about a decade of servitude?" Ander let out a nervous laugh as the giant head, now the size of an elephant, burst through the floor, sending men and women toppling all around him. "No-oo?"

There was nothing else to do but flee. Waving a hand at the wall of the villa, Ander blasted the side out of it and, projecting himself through it, flew out the hole and floated himself safely many feet away, right over the heads of a couple of humans who had come to investigate the noise and earthquake.

The two men stared at Ander in all his naked glory, horns bright in the moonlight and eyes glowing with magic, as he came to rest on his feet before them.

"Well, bollocks." There wasn't much else Ander could think to say. Mortals had seen him performing magic, which meant the ignis filled with righteous fury would be setting upon him momentarily.

If it wasn't death by the man-eating husband, it would be being bound and locked away by Underworld's all too rigorous warriors.

As if sensing their cue, the beat of wings sounded in the air, and a dark shadow fell over Ander. Looking up, he could see the expansive wingspan of first one, then two ignis soldiers flying overhead.

"Double bullocks." He looked back to the humans in front of him. "Can we just pretend that you haven't seen me tonight?"

The humans, still speechless, just shook their heads.

The two ignis, taller and broader than any beings had a right to be, landed lightly on their sandaled feet, swords strapped to their thighs and metal armor over their chests. With their wings folded up against their backs, they towered over both him and the two humans.

"Listen, it was a matter of life or death." His words were only compounded by the explosion of Erotes, in giant form, through the side of the villa. White stone went soaring through the air, and one of the ignis lifted his shield to protect the humans from harm.

Ander took this as his moment to flee, and as he turned on his heel to run, a carriage suddenly pulled up before him, and the door was thrown open.

Perhaps the most beautiful man he'd ever laid eyes on peered down at him from the carriage door. "Did you call for an escape?"

Ander, smiling brilliantly, only managed a hurried, "Yes please!" before clambering in and letting the unexpected hero whisk him away. Turning to watch the fiasco behind him, he saw Erotes bellow in fury and attempt to come after them, only to be halted by the two winged soldiers blocking his way.

A rampaging giant god making his way through the village was far worse than a horned half-muse escaping by carriage.

"By the gods, thank you." Ander collapsed back against the seat of the carriage, blowing his bangs out of his sight as he turned his head to look at his dark-eyed savior.

"You seemed like you could use the help, Ander Ruin."

Ander looked at him in surprise, trying to decide if he actually knew the man or not, but came up short. "This hardly seems fair. You know who I am, but I don't know who you are."

"Underworld knows me as Orcus, but here in the human realm, they call me Enrique."

The name Orcus sent a shiver down Ander's spine. He knew who Orcus was, though he had never laid eyes on him before. The right hand of Hades. The punisher of broken oaths. Otherwise known as the man in charge of torturing those locked away in Hades' dungeons. He had no right being this gorgeous.

"Enrique suits you." And it did. He appeared as if he had been born somewhere in the depths of Spain. Loved by the sun and sculpted by Michelangelo himself. Thick dark brows sat over bottomless dark eyes, a proud nose, angled jaw, and a set of full lips that begged to be kissed. If Ander weren't already sitting down, he'd have taken a seat.

"Thank you." He flashed him a smile. "Where to?"

"Well, I have a feeling Greece isn't going to be the most welcoming place for me for a while. How do you feel about Barcelona?"

"I love Barcelona."

Barcelona, Spain

Draping a silk robe he'd bought in China around himself, Ander left his bathing room and stepped into his bedroom only to find Enrique setting a bottle of champagne on the nightstand and the room aglow with candles. It was breathtaking, and it sent tingles over his skin.

When the two of them had arrived back at his villa, Ander had thought Enrique would be keen on tumbling him into bed as a thank you for getting him out of the trouble he'd been in. Instead, the other man drew him a heated bath full of scented oils and flower petals and then left Ander to soak in it.

"What have we here?"

Enrique looked over at him in the doorway and smiled slowly. "I thought after all of tonight's excitement you may be tired. Relaxing in bed with a glass of champagne seemed like the best way to fall asleep."

"Really?" This surprised Ander. "Will you be joining me?"

"I was hoping you'd ask me to."

In response, Ander held out his hand and tugged him to the plush bed covered in silk and pillows.

They then lay in bed, wrapped up in each other's arms, drinking champagne and talking until the sun came up. At last, when the birds began to chirp outside his window, Enrique leaned in to kiss him deeply, causing that tingle from earlier to resurface and travel all the way down to his toes.

"You're beautiful. Even more so with the sunlight shining on your skin." Enrique's fingers traveled over the flesh of his bare chest. "Do the mortals mistake you as someone from the orient?"

"Mm, yes. I'm seen as exotic and rare."

"You are," Enrique breathed out, then promptly kissed him again.

The kissing led to touching, which developed into thorough lovemaking that left Ander whimpering and exhausted, curled up in Enrique's arms.

At last, he fell asleep, feeling safe and content.

The Sea of Clotho, Underworld
August 1860

Sophelia was mind-numbingly dull. Mab wasn't sure what she had expected from a monastery. Maybe she had thought that such a place in Underworld would be different. That it would offer more than just bland food and even blander conversation—when there was any. But that wasn't what surprised her most about her time in Sophelia.

No, what surprised her the most was just how much she missed Ander's company.

He was a pain in the ass, that was true, but over the years they had been traveling together, he had become family. Yes, he got them into all manner of trouble. Yes, Mab always had to pull them out of it before that trouble became fatal—the incident in France played through her mind, making her simultaneously annoyed and amused at how they had almost been shot by an angry mob—but he kept things interesting.

Maybe if it had just been the boredom of the place, Mab

would have been able to deal with it. She'd dealt with tedium for years at a time in the asylum. A little boredom wouldn't kill her.

It isn't just the boredom, though, she thought, rolling over in a cold sweat for the third night in a row, tightly wound white curls sticking to her skin and her heart hammering so quickly in her chest that it made her nauseous. Mab blinked up at the ceiling, trying to get her breathing under control.

"You're not there anymore, Mabbers," Ander would have said. "You're safe, with me."

Then he would have wrapped her up against his chest and told her to match his breathing until the panic had faded into something that was manageable. It never truly went away. She lived with it every day, like a buzz under her skin. But with Ander, she'd learned to deal with it because he'd always been there. Even when he had a lover over, if she needed him, he was there. He'd more than once pushed whoever it was out of his bed and told them to stay in one of the guest rooms, just to give Mab the time she needed to feel safe again.

He wasn't there now. It was just her and the figures that lurked in the shadows. Her and the memories of the screams. They echoed. The shadows stretched. The stone ceiling of the room looked more and more familiar. The constant *drip drip drip* of water drowned out the sound of her own heart.

"You're not there anymore, Mabbers," she told herself, hugging herself tightly enough that her arms ached. "You're safe."

She didn't feel safe. She didn't think she'd ever feel safe again. She needed to go *home.*

Rolling from her bed, she moved to dig through the

trunk at the end of it where Cassia had told her to store her "worldly" clothes. Her fingers grazed the midnight-blue robes that lay atop the dress she'd come in almost longingly. A silent wish that she'd been able to find the peace in Sophelia that seemed so easy for all the others. There was no peace to be found in this place, not for her.

Cassia was easy to find once Mab had packed what little she needed to take with her. The woman was sitting in the middle of the courtyard garden, her legs curled beneath her as she stared up at the fading stars.

"You are leaving us," Cassia said before Mab could even say a word.

"I am." Mab moved to stand in front of her, watching Cassia's face for any sign of what she was thinking. There was none. Cassia's expression remained impassive and free of judgment.

"I thought this might happen." Cassia lowered her chin so that she could look at Mab and stood from her seat. "I have already made arrangements for your return trip to the mortal world. I am sorry you could not stay longer."

"Me too." Mab shrugged. It only felt a little like a lie. She did *want* to fit in in Sophelia with others of her kind. It was just . . . Well, who was watching Ander's back when she wasn't there?

"You can come back any time." Cassia smiled reassuringly, holding a hand out to Mab to guide her back inside. "I have prepared a talisman that you can use whenever you decide to rejoin us. It will lead you back to Sophelia. You won't be able to find us without it."

Mab's fingers trembled as she took the tiny ceramic turtle. Its shell was painted to look like the night sky, and its eyes were closed to give it a calm expression. A look of acceptance and understanding that Mab had only ever seen on the women in Sophelia. "How do you know I'll come back?"

"They always come back." Cassia's smile only grew, as if she knew something Mab didn't. "I wish you fortune in finding whatever it is you're searching for, Sister Mab."

"Thank you."

Barcelona, Spain - September 1860

Mab didn't think Ander would still be where she left him. In all the years she'd known him, he had never stayed in one place long. But she hoped that he'd left a forwarding address or a note behind, so that she could find him when she returned. What she hadn't thought would happen when she knocked was for the door to fling open and the person answering to shout an excited, "Mabbers!"

Crushed against Ander's chest in a hug so tight it made her ribs ache, Mab felt safe for the first time in months. Gods, she had missed this. The easy companionship. The casual touches. The way Ander was just there when she needed someone, just as he'd been all those years ago at the pyre.

"Oh gods, I have so much to tell you, Mabbers." He laughed, high and bright, pulling back only to grab her hands and tug her through the door into the small foyer of their villa. "But first, we must go shopping. You cannot keep wearing that . . . Well, I hesitate to call it a dress, in a new season. Come, come. We'll get you something fabulous."

"Can I sit my bags down before you drag me out to the

stores?" Mab huffed, feigning annoyance and swallowing down the words she likely should have told him.

"Oh, if you must." And just like that, they were back to how they'd been months ago.

Mab just shook her head and made her way up to her room, which was, remarkably, exactly the same as she had left it but didn't smell musty or closed up at all. She smiled to herself and dropped her bag on the bed.

"When we get back from shopping, I have someone I want you to meet," Ander said from where he leaned against the doorframe.

"Oh? Your flavor of the week?"

Ander laughed, the sound ringing out and filling the room with warmth. It drew a small chuckle from Mab's throat.

The laughter died away, and Ander shook his head. "No . . . No, I dare say Enrique is more than a flavor of the week."

Mab turned to him, her brows raised, but Ander didn't answer the unspoken question. He spun to go back out into the hall. "Come on, we're wasting prime shopping hours."

"All right." She nodded and followed behind him.

Fabric swished around Mab's ankles as she held back her hair, looking at herself in the mirror. Pistachio wasn't exactly her favorite color, but Ander swore up and down this was the shade of the season. As if she cared.

"Well? Let's see it," Ander called, giving the curtain a threatening little tug.

"Hold your horses, Andy." Mab let out a hard breath

that blew a loose curl away from her face. The man at the shop had tried to force her into a corset, but with one irritable look from Ander, he'd relented.

"Darling, never."

Mab snorted and opened the curtain.

"Oh, sir, you were right. Your wife didn't need the corset at all," the salesman said, his hands clapping happily.

"She's not my wife." Ander blanched, an accompanying shudder of revulsion running down Mab's spine.

"That's disgusting," Mab muttered. The idea of being married to Ander was appalling. Likewise was the fact that people who didn't know them always seemed to assume they were engaged and not siblings.

"Leave us alone, Cristobel. We don't need your help anymore." Ander flicked his wrist at the man, and Mab thanked the gods when he took the hint and scuttled away to bother someone else across the tiny shop.

Ander took Mab's hand and forced her to do a little twirl for him. "You look ravishing in that color, darling. I could never. It'd just make me look like a fat ol' pea."

Mab wrinkled her nose at the comment. She'd never heard Ander call himself fat before, not even jokingly. He was always confident and sure. He knew his worth. Something about it was . . . off to her. Like the words were parroted from someone else. "We should find you something while we're here too. I don't want to be the only one getting new things."

"Oh, no. Not right now." Ander laughed, shaking his head. "I'm afraid I've got a couple of pounds to shed before I can even think about anything new in my wardrobe."

"What?" Mab stopped where she'd been headed toward the men's racks to find Ander a new waistcoat. Something in the same color that she knew would set off his skin tone just so.

"Come, let's look at what they have in red." Ander grabbed her wrist and dragged her back toward the other racks, his fingers just this side of too tight around the bone.

"All right."

"Mab, I've heard so much about you." Enrique smiled charmingly, the expression wrinkling his face in all the right places, almost too perfectly. Like it was fiction. A made-up story meant to lull children to sleep.

"And I've heard exactly nothing about you," Mab said, her lips pursed a little.

Enrique laughed, the sound booming with mirth and joy, and showing off annoyingly white teeth. "Oh, she's just as funny as you said, princeling."

"I knew you two would get on." Ander preened a little under Enrique's obvious approval, color rising high on his cheeks in delight. Happiness had settled into his features the likes of which Mab hadn't seen before. Not since she'd talked him down off that cliff all those years ago. Maybe . . . just maybe, Enrique would be good for him. The strangeness of his perfection aside.

"You have to come with us tomorrow to Lord Delacruz's party." Enrique leaned forward, his eyes alight with friendliness. "We'll have a wonderful time."

"What's the dress code?" Mab wrinkled her nose.

"Oh, don't worry about that. I'll find you something appropriate to wear. It's the least I can do for my princeling's best friend." Enrique shook his head. "You leave it to me, I'll take care of everything."

"Trust him, Mabbers. He's got exquisite taste," Ander cooed, leaning more heavily into Enrique's side.

"If you insist." Mab shrugged, finishing off the last of her whiskey.

"I do." Enrique rose, taking her empty glass and moving to the bar to refill it. "Maybe we all ought to match. We'd surely throw all of Barcelona into a tizzy walking in together if we did. The three most beautiful people in Spain."

"I don't know about all of Spain." Mab snorted, rolling her eyes.

"Well, I do." Enrique set her glass in front of her, a glint in his gaze that seemed . . . She didn't know what it seemed. She couldn't pinpoint it. And that, more than anything, was what drove her silence. "A toast. To new friends and the most beautiful people in all of Spain." He lifted his glass, that picture-perfect smile back in place.

Mab hesitated for only a moment before Ander's expectant look had her lifting her glass and clinking it against both of theirs. "To new friends."

Chapter 9
Ander

October 1860

From the outside, the villa looked like any other home along the stretch of Spanish soil, but once inside, it was a riotous affair of Underworld citizens. Fenrik's home was an in-between place: one of the earthen locations that was simultaneously located in Underworld as well. It made travel between the realms incredibly easy. One stepped off the streets of an Earth-bound city, and walked through another door into Underworld herself.

"Why don't you and Mab find us a table, and I will grab each of us a plate of food from the buffet?" Enrique offered.

"Thank you, darling. Don't forget lots of those honey cakes Fenrik's chef always makes. They're delicious, and Mab and I love them!" Ander kissed the corner of his lips, then took Mab's arm to lead her across the villa's courtyard to the scattering of tables.

Dining was happening al fresco tonight, and Ander was loving the thought of spending time with his two favorite people. On their way to an empty table, Ander swiped three glasses of champagne off a satyr's tray and set them carefully on the glittery tablecloth before claiming a seat.

"Isn't Enri amazing? I've never been courted by someone so thoughtful before." He leaned back in his chair, tugging at the purple waistcoat he wore.

"Right. Thoughtful," Mab replied dryly.

Ander looked at her, a dark brow lifting in question. "What does that mean?"

"Nothing at all." Mab picked up her champagne glass and downed half of it.

Before he could push the matter, Enrique reappeared, one of Fenrik's satyrs following behind him with three plates. "I have returned with sustenance." He smiled that smile at Ander that turned his knees to jelly and made his heart flutter uncontrollably.

As Enrique took the plates one by one from the satyr and set them before them on the table, Ander couldn't help but note his bore mostly fruit and vegetable slices, with one stuffed grape leaf. Opening his lips to tell Enrique he'd forgotten his honey cakes, he caught Enrique's eye and stopped.

"I got you only the lighter things, as I know you're hoping to go for your new winter wardrobe soon." Enrique reached out to brush fingers gently along his jaw.

Ander smiled softly and nodded. "Thank you for thinking of that."

Mab snorted, which turned into a cough, her fist coming up to rest against her chest. "I seem to be choking on something. Tastes a lot like bull—"

"Prince Ander! Master Orcus! How wonderful to see you both tonight." Fenrik was a giant of a creature, standing at seven feet tall, with broad horns on top of his bull's head and equally broad shoulders that tapered down to a thick waist and muscular thighs. The minotaur, while not one to anger, was also a great champion of throwing a good fete. Ander had attended many a dinner party held by Fenrik and had enjoyed every one.

"Thank you for the invite, Fenrik." Enrique settled back in his seat, his lean body draped in a black velvet robe tied around the waist by a thick gold rope.

"Oh, it was nothing. I always know I'm in for a fabulous night when the prince of Helicon graces my halls. Please, do make sure to thoroughly enjoy yourselves tonight."

"Well, with that welcome, how could we not!" Ander chirped. He eyed Mab. "See, some people do want me to misbehave." He stuck his tongue out at her, then winked.

Enrique cleared his throat and patted Ander's thigh, which brought a blush to his cheeks. Looking over at him, Ander whispered, "Sorry."

He was consoled when Enrique leaned over to press a kiss beneath his ear and murmured to him softly, "Let's have fun tonight, beautiful. I want to see you shine out there on the dance floor."

Wanting to feel a connection with him in this moment, Ander hopped up from his chair. "Let's dance now!" He held his hand out to Enrique, then paused. Maybe Enrique didn't wish to dance just yet. He *had* just arrived with their food. Ander's shoulders relaxed when his beau accepted the offered hand and stood.

"Let's go, my pretty princeling. Mab." Enrique bowed his head to her in an acknowledgement of farewell, to which Mab simply waved her hand with a grunt.

Ander sent her a little smile. "We'll be back!"

"Yeah, yeah."

Out on the patch of cobblestone left empty of tables and nearest the musicians, Ander wound his arms around

Enrique's neck and allowed himself to be drawn in against the other man's firm chest. As Enrique's hands settled possessively on his waist, a thrill went through Ander. His hands were strong and contained a heat that branded his flesh everywhere they touched. It hadn't been very long that they had known each other, but Ander already felt as if Enrique owned him down to the very essence of his soul.

Dancing in Underworld was far more physical and sensual than what the human world deemed appropriate; Ander preferred it by far.

November 1860

"Are you almost ready, darling?"

"Just fixing my hair!" Ander called back. Seated at his dressing table, he was desperately trying to naturally restrain a wayward strand of hair before he finally gave up and used magic to coif his hair how he wanted it.

"We were supposed to be there on the hour. It's now half past," Enrique said, coming into the bedroom.

"So sorry, Enri, but I'm all ready now!" He stood up and twirled to face Enrique, showing himself off, only to stop, the smile slipping from his face. Enrique was looking at him in a puzzled manner. "What? What's wrong?"

"Nothing . . . it's nothing."

"No, tell me."

"Well, it's just, this is the first time you're meeting Sophocles, and I want you to impress him."

Ander's shoulders fell, an anxious feeling settling in his

stomach and making his heart tighten. "What's wrong with what I'm wearing?" Self-consciously, his hands ran down over his chest.

Enrique was taking him to meet one of his closest confidants from Underworld. Someone he worked closely with each time he returned to Hades' domain to fulfill his godly duties. Ander had dressed in one of his loveliest togas. Made from a handwoven silk he'd found at a small market in China, it was a rich royal blue with a gold dragon coiling across it. He'd put it on because he cherished this piece, which reminded him of a wonderful trip with Mab in their early years together.

He had thought it would be the perfect piece to bolster his confidence while meeting Sophocles. *Don't cry.* There was something about displeasing Enrique that always struck Ander to his very core. Perhaps it was that, deep down, he knew he was not worthy of the god.

"It's lovely." Enrique must have sensed that Ander was close to tears because he moved forward to cup his face tenderly between his hands, tipping his chin up so they were looking into each other's eyes. "*You* are lovely, and normally I wouldn't care what you wore, but I really want you to impress Sophocles. You know how some people see you. You've gained quite the reputation around Underworld, and it's hard for most to take you seriously. And Sophocles is simply so particular about things. I just want him to like you as much as I do. Do you have anything perhaps a little subtler?"

Subtle. The word shouldn't hurt, and yet it did.

Clearing his throat, Ander blinked away the tears and nodded. "I can do subtle. I have a more traditional toga."

Enrique grinned brilliantly, and it made the pain lessen. "You're fabulous." He leaned in and kissed him soundly. "Now hurry, being late won't help your case any."

Feeling dazed by the kiss, Ander only nodded and hurried into his closet to quickly change his clothes.

When he came back out, Enrique kissed his fingertips. "Absolute perfection!"

Ander beamed and danced into his arms, laughing as Enrique twirled him across the floor, pressing several more kisses to his lips. "No one will ever love you like I love you," Enrique purred against his cheek. "You are mine, Ander Ruin."

Ander shivered at the words and let Enrique lead him off to the gentlemen's club that would take them into Underworld.

London, England - December 1860

"What about this one?" Mab held up a roll of fabric.

The crimson satin was just the shade of lustrous that Ander typically fell all over. It screamed sex, seduction, and a good time. He wanted nothing more than to run his hands over the fabric and feel it draped over his naked flesh.

"No, not that one." He turned away from it quickly before he could be further tempted.

"Huh?" Mab gazed after him in confusion. "But you love red. It's your favorite color."

"I'm just not feeling it right now. I think I'll go with this soft lilac, it's more the tone I expect to see this social season." Along with the bolt of lilac, he also picked up a bolt of navy.

"You're not feeling it, or *Enri* doesn't like it?" Her face twisted as she said his name, like she'd been fed a spoonful of vinegar.

Ander sighed. "Is there something wrong with dressing in a palette my boyfriend approves of?"

"*Approves* of? Yes! Since when did you need approval from *anyone* to do what you want?"

Glaring over at her, Ander dropped the bolts of fabric onto the counter heavily. "I thought you'd be pleased to know that I was trying to tone down my behavior and present myself more becomingly. You're the one who yelled at me for getting us chased out of France!"

The tailor's eyes shot up into his brows, but he quickly schooled his features. "Shirts out of these fabrics, sir?"

"Yes, please," Ander said quickly.

"I love you not getting us chased out of cities anymore, but not at the expense of you forgetting who you are!"

"I'm not forgetting who I am, I'm trying to become a better version of myself." Ander turned to Henry. "You have my measurements. I'll pick them up in a week." Turning from the counter, he leaned in closer to Mab. "I thought as my best friend you would understand what I'm trying to do. Enri loves me, and I want to be the best version of myself for him."

"Best version? Ander, there was nothing wrong—"

"Is something the matter?" Enrique's voice sounded from the door of the tailor shop. Ander hadn't even heard the bell ring.

"Not at all," Ander responded, shooting him a forced smile. "I was just leaving." He stepped up to Enrique and slipped an arm through his.

"Wonderful, I've made us dinner reservations." Enrique offered his arm to Mab as well.

"No thank you," she snipped. "I'm not feeling terribly hungry." Her eyes bore into Ander, but he looked away.

He hated it when he and Mab fought. She was the closest thing he had to family when he was in the mortal world. But he'd never had a lover who *wanted* to remain at his side. Typically, they were long gone by now, but not this one. No, Enrique had stayed. Loved him, even. It felt like a miracle, the answer to a long-ago question. *Could anyone ever?*

Chapter 10
Mab

He was too thin. Mab hadn't noticed it as it was happening —although, now she was wondering how she could have possibly missed it—but then, she had gone to Ireland to check on the manor for a fortnight and come home to find Ander sitting at the breakfast table picking at a bowl of fruit and all at once, it caught up with her. He was too thin.

His skin looked paler than she thought she'd ever seen it. And his cheeks, which had always been angular, looked just this side of sunken. The housecoat he wore hung almost limply off his shoulders, like there wasn't enough of him to keep it from slipping to the floor.

How could Mab have missed it? He was her best friend. Her family. And she had missed the warning signs completely.

No.

Not *missed* them, she reasoned. She'd noticed the way Enrique seemed to want to control every aspect of Ander's life. How he always made sure to get Ander's plate for him at parties. How he nitpicked everything that Ander wore until eventually Ander had given up and begun to think only of wearing what Enrique might approve of. *Approve.* Not appreciate. Not find most attractive. Not like. But give his consent to see Ander in. Like Ander needed permission to simply exist at all. It turned her stomach.

Swallowing roughly, Mab pulled a smile onto her face that felt more rictus than sincere, Ander didn't seem to notice. "Why don't you get dressed, and we'll go round to that patisserie we like so well. I'm sure they'll have some of those lemon blueberry scones." She wiggled her eyebrows enticingly.

"No. I'm not particularly hungry." Ander nibbled at the corner of a piece of melon.

Mab took a breath and resisted the urge to roll her eyes and snap at Ander. It wouldn't help. It'd just make him defensive. She knew that well enough. She didn't want a repeat of their argument a couple of months back at the tailor's. But Mab had made up her mind when she'd come home to London last week and seen him like this: she was going to discuss this with Ander. She was going to try to extricate him from Enrique's influence if she could. Or at least minimize the damage he was able to do by making Ander aware of it.

"Then let's go for a walk. Come, the fresh air will do us both some good," she pressed, smearing her toast in a bit of honey.

"Mabbers, it's positively frigid out. We're not going for a walk." Ander dropped the piece of melon so he could fix her with raised brows. "What's this about?"

There was a creak on the stair behind Ander, and Mab's eyes shifted to see the shadow of someone against the wall.

Her shoulders pulled taught enough to strain her neck. "Nothing. It's nothing."

"All right," Ander said, his brow knitted in confusion. The shadow receded, but Mab had little doubt that Enrique had heard her. She'd have to be more careful.

London, England - March 1861

Over the following weeks, Enrique clung to Ander like the rancid smell of a pig pen. There was not a moment where Mab could catch Ander alone to broach the subject with him, and she became increasingly uncomfortable with what that meant. It wasn't until, as the season finally seemed to be turning and they took their first stroll in the warm almost-spring air, things finally came to a head.

"I was thinking, Mabbers," Ander said, his arm looped through hers on one side and Enrique's on the other, like an uncomfortable daisy chain, "perhaps when we make our next move, you ought to find your own house."

"What?" Mab squeaked, her step stuttering so that, for a moment, Ander was almost dragging her along the little path. She caught up a second later, but she could see the way her faltered step troubled her friend.

"It could be next door, mind you," Enrique offered. As if that made this discussion any less upsetting, lessened the blow at all. It did not.

"Why?" Mab asked on a breath. She was suddenly running out of air. Drowning, she was *drowning*. Of course, she'd been away from Ander before. For months when she'd been in Sophelia, and two weeks in Ireland. That was different. As selfish as it was, on those few occasions, she'd always known she could come back home. She'd always known that Ander would be waiting for her. This wasn't like that. This was . . . this was like Enrique was taking Ander away from her. Severing the bond they'd forged over the last couple of decades.

"We thought it might be nice to have a little more privacy," Ander said, his voice soft and gentle, like he was breaking news to a child, but the words didn't sound like his. It sounded like he was one of those creepy dummies they'd once seen at the theater. Enrique's voice thrown into Ander's mouth to make it seem like it was all Ander's idea when, clearly, it was not. Ander had never needed privacy before. Not like that.

"We'll help you find someplace, of course," Enrique pressed on, his tone implying that the matter was settled completely. He would be brokering no arguments. Not from Ander, and certainly not from Mab.

Mab wasn't sure what she said after that, her mind a swarming buzz of upset that she could hardly think through. Their walk continued. Enrique and Ander's voices washed over her, but she could feel Ander's eyes on her, searching and worried. He let the subject lie, at least for the time being, but Mab was not a fool. She knew they'd be coming back to it when there were less ears.

She was proven right some hours later when Ander cornered her in the receiving room, a glass of scotch in his hand and an expectant look on his face. "A peace offering."

"I didn't know we were at war," she said but took the glass anyway and gulped down a healthy swallow from it in preparation for the conversation to come. She wondered where Enrique had disappeared to and when he'd be back.

Or was he still there? Lurking somewhere out of sight so he could overhear everything she told Ander and reappear in enough time to assert his dominance over the situation once more.

"I apologize for springing that on you earlier." Ander took a dainty sip from his own glass—a habit he'd acquired since Enrique—that made Mab's eyebrow twitch.

"I suppose there's nothing I can say to change your mind on the matter?" She had to ask. Even if she already knew the answer, Mab had to ask. If she could have just put this conversation off for a bit longer. Drag out the relative stalemate she and Enrique seemed to have. But no. He was not going to allow that. He was going to force her hand. And she could only hope that in doing so, he was going to see that he'd overestimated the control he had over Ander, underestimated the connection they shared.

"No, there is not." Ander moved to settle onto the settee with her, taking her hand in his and giving it a firm squeeze. "This is for the best, Mabbers. Enri's right, it's time for you to step out on your own at least a little."

Mab almost laughed. The sound caught like wet paper in her throat. She wanted to cry. She wanted to sob. She wanted to *scream*. She wanted to grab her dear friend—her only family—by the shoulders and shake him until his teeth rattled. Until he saw how wrong he was. Until he realized how much he was hurting her by hurting himself. Instead, she downed the rest of her scotch and clutched the glass so tightly, she swore it would crack under her grip.

"I'm not leaving you alone with him." Her voice left her a broken, raw thing, all banshee—the ruined sound of it a carryover from her wailing on the pyre, that she often hid by modulating her tone to put the mortals they surrounded themselves with at ease.

"What?" Ander frowned, his eyes going impossibly wide in his too-thin face.

"I won't. I *can't.*"

"What do you mean?" He took another dainty sip from his drink, likely to hide the subtle tremble of his fingers from the coming confrontation, but she saw it. She'd always see it. Because she knew him. Because she loved him.

"I mean that if anyone is moving out, it's *Enrique.*" The last word tasted like venom on her tongue, so much so, she spat it more than spoke it. "Can't you see it, Andy? Can't you see what he's doing to you? You've been a shadow of yourself for *months*! And for what? I can't—*I won't* sit by any longer and watch you fade away as you are."

"You don't know what you're talking about." Ander pulled himself up straighter, his chin tilting back.

"I don't, do I?" Mab reached for his wrist, yanking it up so they could both see in the warm firelight just how thin his arms had gotten under his sleeves. The skin pulled almost too tight across the bone in a garish mockery of how he'd once looked. She remembered clinging to him when she'd had nightmares during those first years. She remembered his strong arms holding her together when it felt like she'd break apart into too many tiny pieces to ever be whole again. These arms couldn't do that. These arms could barely hold up the bloody glass currently gripped in his fingers. "I know what hunger feels like, Andy. What being on the brink of starvation does to a person. When was the last time you didn't feel that gnawing ache in your belly? When was the last time you actually enjoyed a meal? And don't get me started on your clo—"

"You're just jealous!" Ander spat, yanking his arm from her, the words landing like a slap across her face.

"Excuse me?" Mab reeled back, her heart stuttering in

her chest.

"I said you're jealous. Because you don't have anyone, because you *haven't* had anyone since I've known you." There was so much venom and spite in his tone that she hardly recognized him as the man she'd begun to call brother.

"I'm not jealous of that . . . that . . . that abusive, manipulative, *bastard*!"

"You are," Ander crowed, a victory. "You're jealous because you don't have me all to yourself anymore. Because no one loves you like Enri loves me. And how could they when you don't—"

"Fine!" Mab stood, smacking her glass so hard on the table in front of the settee that she heard something crack. "If that's what you think, then fine! He can keep you. Let yourself wither away to nothing! But don't come crying to me when he discards you like the object he sees you as."

She didn't wait for him to respond. She stormed from the room, from the townhouse entirely, out into the busy city streets of the early evening. It took her a handful of blocks before her heart stopped slamming against the walls of her chest. And another three before she finally realized how rash she'd been. She was at Hyde Park by the time she'd resolved to go back and apologize, and she turned around to make the trek home.

Except when she reached it, the house was quiet as a grave. No softly crackling fire. No sound of Ander milling about. Nothing. She rushed up the stairs to Ander and Enrique's room and found the wardrobe thrown open and emptied, the bathroom free of Ander's ridiculous toiletries, and not even a note to say where they had gone.

They had just . . . they had just *left*. Just like that.

And Mab Duchan was alone, in London, again.

Chapter 11
Ander

Acheron, Underworld – May 1861

The sun was shining in Acheron; bright rays disappearing into the depths of Tartarus' smoky billows and dancing over the crystal forest of Elysium. While a part of Underworld, Acheron was also a land unto itself, almost a world within a world. Here was where the dead of Underworld ended up. It gave Ander the shivers whenever he thought on it.

A few of the servants were currently in the courtyard, tossing pitchers of water at each other in an attempt to cool off in a rare moment of levity in the terrifying landscape of punishment and suffering. Their laughter filtered up through the open window, and the empty spot inside Ander's chest ached more profoundly. He used to laugh like that almost every day: carefree outings to parties, scandalous behavior wherever he went, a devoted friend who was always there to share in the joke.

"You could join them, Your Highness." The voice was soft and encouraging as it spoke behind him, causing Ander to startle and jump. "If you wished to."

Ander turned in his spot on the window seat, looking at the young satyr standing before him. "Please . . . just Ander. I hate the formal title."

"Lord Orcus has insisted we be respectful of your position, Your Hi—"

Ander held up his hand, halting any further words. "I know, but perhaps when he's not around, it could be just Ander?" he asked hopefully. The title felt like it belonged to someone else. It distanced him from everyone he had any chance of coming into contact with here.

There weren't many Acheron civilians lining up to befriend the horned prince sitting like a prized poodle in the black fortress belonging to Hades, king of Acheron, god of the dead, and brother to Indra of Olympia.

"If that is what you wish, Your—Ander." The servant bit his lip, shifting anxiously on his feet.

"Do you think they would be fine with me joining in with them out there?" He could hear the desperate hope in his own voice, and inwardly, he cringed.

There was nothing to do during the day until Enrique returned from his duties, which kept him busy from morning to night. Once he was finished, their evenings were spent together. Dining. Drinking. Making love until Ander could no longer breathe. For those few hours each night, it was glorious, and Ander came alive.

But the days were solitary and empty.

"Of course they would. They all like you very much."

Ander's face split with a large grin, and he bounced eagerly to his feet. "Well then, let's go and get drenched!"

The one wonderful thing about being a muse was the magic that flowed endlessly through his body and made it so that he didn't have to waste time on silly things like hallways and staircases. Instead, Ander snapped his fingers, and instantly, he was outside beneath the scorching sunshine, standing barefoot on sizzling black pumice stone.

Several gasped, "Your Highness!" as he appeared to disturb their games.

"Please, don't stop on my account." Grinning, Ander produced a pitcher of water, which he promptly threw upon the closest female, who shrieked, then broke into delighted laughter.

Soon, Ander, too, was entirely soaked from head to foot, his pale blue toga clinging to his thin frame. As the waves of water flew through the air, the loneliness melted away beneath the hot sun and was washed away with each new pitcher thrown.

He'd just received a bucketful to the face, which left him laughing and coughing, when a deep baritone called his name. His heart skipped a beat, while his stomach knotted sickeningly. Wiping his face clean, Ander turned on his heel to face Enrique.

With one crook of his finger, the god of punishment had Ander scurrying to his side as the servants bowed around him.

"Ander, dearest, what are you doing?" His voice was low, saving Ander the embarrassment of being scolded in front of the help.

"I was bored," he whispered, biting at his bottom lip, "and hot. This seemed like a good idea at the time."

Enrique took his hand in a firm grip, leading him away from the wet stones of the courtyard and back into the fortress. "But perhaps not appropriate, considering who you were committing such actions with?" Enrique's brow lifted in question.

"Well, I—"

"You're the Crown Prince of Helicon, Ander. I know

you don't much care for that position, but while you can be whomever you wish on Earth, here in Underworld, you need to respect that role."

Ander frowned down at the floor as they walked, wishing to wiggle his fingers in the clutch that was making them go numb but not daring to. "I wasn't thinking."

"Well, that is obvious. And constant." Enrique sighed, then stopped in his tracks, halting Ander. The hand not gripping Ander's lifted to cup his cheek, tipping his head back so he met his gaze. "I don't want to argue. I love your playful side. You know I do." He leaned in to kiss Ander's lips. "But this is Acheron, and here, we live beneath Hades' rule. Please don't embarrass me in front of him."

Ander flushed deeply in shame, wishing the ground would open up and swallow him whole, tugging him down into the pits of lava Enrique used to torture and punish his designated dead. "I'm sorry, Enri. I'll make better decisions next time. I promise."

Enrique smiled brilliantly down at him, and that tightness in his stomach eased a little. "I know you will, princeling."

Then their lips were together once more, and Enrique's arms were around him, holding him firmly against his chest despite the wet fabric pressed between them. The contact made Ander's head swim and his knees feel weak as he let his lover sweep him away by sheer force.

"I love you," Ander murmured against his lips.

Enrique smiled and pressed another soft kiss to his lips. "Come with me, I have a surprise for you."

"Oh?" Ander perked up, despite the pang in his heart. In this moment, he'd needed to hear the words back, but he would accept Enrique's attention instead. "Show me!"

Enrique laughed and led him through the hallways of

Fortress Ploutos, up one of the grand staircases, and into the wing that contained their chambers. Inside their quarters, he found a sea of clothing awaiting him in dark gem tones.

"Surprise! I told you new clothes were coming. Finally, some proper items to truly make your beauty stand out, rather than all those terrible mortal realm pieces."

Ander surveyed the yards and yards of silk, satins, and linen. "Enri, this is amazing. Thank you so much." He turned to throw his arms around him, pressing kisses to his face.

Strong arms slid around his waist, holding him trapped against his chest. "You deserve it. After all the hard work you've done to sculpt yourself into the perfect vision of beauty for me, I wanted to reward you."

"You're the best."

The next kiss was hungry, powerful, all-consuming. Ander was overcome, the very essence of himself disappearing into the burning flame that was Enrique.

Tumbling down onto their bed, he bared himself to the onslaught of Enrique's hands and mouth, coming undone beneath his ministrations. Being remade by the force of his thrusts inside him. Breaking into a million little, irreparable pieces until there was nothing left but a shadow of what had once been.

June 1861

"I think perhaps I should reach out to Mab."

Enrique paused in the middle of lifting a boiled egg to

his lips and peered across the table at him. "What brought this on? I thought we agreed in London that you two needed time apart. She wasn't okay with our relationship and you being happily committed to someone that wasn't her. *You're* the one who suggested a clean break, Ander. Asking us to leave London entirely. Don't be hypocritical now."

"I know . . . I know. I just—" He hadn't thought it through. Ander and Mab never fought. There had been squabbles, and lots of irritated huffing on Mab's part, but never true fights. It had broken Ander's heart in a way nothing since Estelle had. Unable to face it, he'd packed up his things and convinced himself that another townhouse in London wasn't enough, the only solution was fleeing to Underworld with Enrique.

They needed space. Time to figure out who they were without the other person constantly being there.

But did Ander even like who he was without Mab?

How was Mab doing without him there to comfort her during her night terrors? The thought of her waking up shaking and alone made him sick to his stomach. Had she found someone else to hold her through the night? Would she even allow anyone else to?

"You just what?"

"I miss her." The words came out soft and ashamed.

"Why? She was demanding of your personal time and space. She wasn't a friend to you, Ander, she was using you."

His brows pinched together. "No, that's not true."

"No?" Enrique grunted darkly. Tossing his napkin down onto the tabletop, he stood and moved to a dresser nearby. Plucking up a small round mirror from its surface, he muttered a few words in the ancient tongue too soft for

Ander to truly hear, then thrust it in front of him. "Ask it to see Mab."

"What?"

"Ask the mirror to show you Mab," he snapped.

Tentatively taking the mirror from Enrique, Ander looked down at its small reflective surface. "Please show me Mab."

The image of his face dissolved into a swirling vortex until settling into a new vision. It was Mab, vibrant and lively, laughing amongst a group of men and women. He'd never seen her with such a group of people around her before. He wasn't able to hear what was being said, but he could see the captivated look in her companions' eyes. Could see the pure happiness shining from Mab's.

She was living better without him than she'd ever lived with him.

"I didn't want you to see this . . . but you needed to know. She's moved on to others without you, Ander. She's happy. Does it look like she's missing you?"

"No." It came out on a choked sob while he blinked rapidly to keep the tears at bay. She'd never looked happier. Mab didn't miss him. She didn't feel this gaping, agonizing hole inside her where once her best friend had resided.

Perhaps he had been nothing to her. He was never anything to anyone. The only one who seemed to want him as desperately as he wanted them was Enrique.

"She can't ever love you like I do, darling." He combed his fingers through Ander's hair, making sure to avoid the horns on top of his head, lest he accidentally graze one. They were not his favorite thing.

"You're right." Ander swallowed down the tears, clearing his throat. "She's fine without me, and I'm better without her." He took a large gulp of wine, wishing it were something harder. He watched Enrique sit back down to finish his breakfast.

Turning the mirror upside down on the table, Ander stared at his own breakfast—barely touched. Pushing it away, he leaned back in his chair. "So, I think I might go visit Sora today." Enrique made a face at this. "Or maybe not. If you don't think I should."

"You know you can befriend whomever you wish, darling. I just want you to be happy. But we do need to think about what image we're putting forth when we are seen with some people. Sora is nice enough, but she's not well looked upon by high society here."

Ander could only nod, his shoulders slumping. Sora was a sweet winemaker who'd befriended him at a banquet a fortnight ago and had actually made Ander feel at home for the first time since his arrival in Acheron.

"Why don't you go and visit Louba and Sorkis? I know Sophocles would be touched if you spent time with them."

Ander held back a look of distaste, not wanting Enrique to see how he felt about his friends. While they'd accepted him into their circle, Ander always felt less-than in their presence. Sophocles was a warden of the dungeons, a position of great power in Hades' fortress. He had worked for many centuries alongside Enrique. Louba and Sorkis, his lovers, thought very highly of themselves because of the parties they attended due to their partner's connections.

Ander often had the feeling that his royal lineage was the only thing that made him acceptable in their eyes. Everything else about him was something to turn their noses up at, the satyr horns especially.

"Maybe staying home today is for the best. I don't want to intrude on them uninvited."

"Well, you'll have me all to yourself tonight. We can go

out to the Asphodel for our evening meal." Enrique stood up, leaning down to kiss Ander on the forehead before he walked away to dress for the day.

"That sounds . . . wonderful."

Enrique paused, turning back around to look at him. "We don't have to go if you're not excited about it. I just thought you might like a special treat of going out for the evening. Just the two of us."

"Oh no, I love the idea." Ander flashed a bright smile at him. "I can't wait."

Chapter 12
Mab

Moher, Ireland - July 1861

He was fine, Mab told herself.

He was fine.

He was fine.

He was *fine*.

She repeated it like a mantra, but no matter how many times she told herself, it didn't seem to want to stick. It had been damn near six months, and it still didn't seem to want to stick.

Ander had gone willingly, that much was clear. There had been no signs of struggle. He'd simply packed his bag and left with Enrique. Left Mab behind for that . . . that . . . *rat bastard.*

"He's fine. He's probably even happy you're gone," Mab mumbled, but the winds of the cliffs stole the words from her lips, blowing her white hair back from her face. "Happy he can do whatever he wants now without you there to drag him out, or tell him it's a bad idea, or dampen the mood."

It had been a long time since she'd stood on a cliff and

stared out across the sea, likely too long. Not since she'd found Ander standing on cliffs just like these, out of his mind with grief and self-loathing, just looking for a quick and easy way to end it all. She'd pulled him back from the edge then. With a blade of grass and a story about the things she'd found along the way that had made her long life worth living.

There was no one there to pull her back from the edge now, she realized, the toes of her boots hanging off the rocky ledge, the wind at her face, and the water crashing so loud against the stone below, she could hardly hear her own thoughts. No one to remind her that the darkness could only swallow her whole if she let it. No one to hold her, and sing to her, and chase away the shadows that always lingered at the edges of her mind. No one who loved her enough to notice them. If she wanted to jump, she could. She doubted anyone would miss her or even notice she was gone.

But that was the thing—the crux of it, really: she didn't want to jump.

So instead, she crouched carefully and sat on the edge, her boots kicking against the rocky cliffs like those of a child in a chair that was far too tall for them. Mab closed her eyes and breathed in the sea salt air of the ocean, and hoped, prayed to whatever was out there looking after her and Ander, whatever had brought them together in the first place, that he was all right. That he *was* fine. That he was happy, even.

Another deep inhale, forcing the air down into her lungs, pressing hard against her ribs, expanding them until it hurt and the ache of it made her eyes water. Then Mab opened her eyes and moved to stand. But before she could get very far, her head swam. Dizziness would have swayed her forward over the edge if she hadn't stumbled back instead.

Her body thumped hard against the ground, knocking the air from her lungs, and then Mab was in the dark.

Not like she'd lost consciousness but like she was standing in a dark room. The crash of the waves, the bite of the wind, the rustle of the grass—there was none of that wherever Mab was now. Just emptiness that went on and on for eternity.

She blinked, lifting her hands to rub at her eyes. When she pulled them away, the darkness and silence were replaced with the deafening sounds of battle and a light so bright it burned her eyes. It took her a moment to see through the feathers and the dust, but there, burning alive, was Ander Ruin, his face a mask of anguish so raw, it cut her to the bone. She held out her hand, to reach for him, to pull him from the flames just as he had for her all those years ago, but something moved out of the corner of her eyes, drawing her attention away.

Enrique. Blood dripped from his hands. White feathers and viscera clumped on the polished metal of his sword. And he had a crazed look in his eyes. A vicious victory the likes of which she had never seen before.

Ander screamed again, the sound like a heart rending to pieces, and the flames grew hotter, turning blue. He wasn't looking at Enrique. His head turned to stare at something on the other side of him that Mab couldn't see for the flames.

Tears clouded her vision, making it hard to see what was happening, but she had to get to him. She had to save Ander. She had to stop Enrique from finishing what he'd started. Her feet stumbled against the uneven ground, legs like jelly with panic.

Something big and black ran in front of her, knocking her to the dirt as it put itself in between her and Ander. Her body thumped against the earth again, then she was staring up at the gray sky of Moher once more, with not much more than the smell of charred flesh in her nose to remember what she'd seen.

"He's going to kill him," Mab said with such certainty that it reached down to her marrow. Something caught in her lungs. A cough ripped through her, and she hacked, retched, sobbed, until she turned onto her side and vomited up what little she'd eaten that day.

A single white feather fluttered in the breeze, somehow untouched by the bile and sick.

"Enrique's going to kill Ander," she repeated, scrambling to her feet. Then she was running as fast as her legs would carry her back to her horse, back to the town, back to anyone who might help her find Ander before it was too late. "I have to find him."

Helicon, Underworld - July 1861

Finding someone who did not want to be found was a lot harder than Mab thought it would be. She'd found him once before, followed his trail of drunken antics to the cliffs, but this was different. Ander wasn't alone, now, and he wasn't grieving. Before, he hadn't cared at all who saw what or what they had to say because he didn't plan to stick around long enough for it to catch up to him. That wasn't the case now.

"And you're sure? You haven't seen him?" she'd asked for what felt like the millionth time not but a week ago. The panicked feeling that had settled into her bones when she'd had the vision hadn't dissipated or lessened at all. She was frantic with it every minute of every day, making it hard to do anything other than search for her wayward friend.

That was what led her back to Helicon. She had been for a brief stay a few years back. Long enough to meet Queen Aemiliana and realize that, in spite of how much his mother loved him, Ander was deeply uncomfortable in his homeland.

"Mab! How nice to see you," Aemiliana greeted, her arms open wide to offer Mab a hug, a smile spread on her face even as her gaze sought out her missing son.

"I'm not—This isn't a social call, Your Majesty." Mab's ribs were squeezing her lungs, leaving her dizzy and lightheaded, just like the last time Ander had convinced her to wear a corset. There wasn't enough air in the room, and the walls, spacious as the castle might be, were closing in on her.

"What is it? What's happened?" Aemiliana's arms fell, her hands fisting in her skirts.

"He took him," Mab blurted, the words seeming to spring to her tongue in a rush. "He took him, and I don't know where. And none of our friends have seen him. And I couldn't protect him. It was my job to protect him. And I couldn't do it. Because . . . because I was selfish. Because I couldn't see what was right in front of my face. How can you ever forgive me? How can I ever forgive *myself*?!"

Someone's hands were tight on her shoulders, forcing her down into a chair, but the room was dark and spinning, and she couldn't make out their voice as they murmured something soft and soothing, much less their face. It must be

Aemiliana. No one other than the queen and her son had ever treated Mab with such kindness, like she was fragile and she might break.

A glass of water was forced in between her fingers, and though she didn't drink, the cool condensation dripping over her knuckles brought her back to herself.

When Mab was able to focus again, Aemiliana crouched before her, long gauzy skirts pooling on the stone floor. Mab thought to tell Aemiliana to get up, that queens weren't supposed to kneel, that she'd soil her dress, but Aemiliana stopped her with a gentle squeeze to her knees.

"Now, what's happened to my son?" she asked, and Mab told her everything. The whole messy business with Enrique, and how the signs were all there, but she had ignored them for some foolish reason. The vision, all of it. She expected Aemiliana to be furious with her, and she had every right to be. Mab had failed the person she loved the most. But when the story was done, Aemiliana just looked over her shoulder to one of the attendants and ordered, "Prepare the carriage. We're going to Acheron to get my son back."

The horned god, as the mortals called him, was more terrifying in person than Mab would have ever imagined. Not that she had ever really given much thought to the mortals' gods before Ander. They had been lore, fictions made up to scare people into being good, and kind, and humble. But Hades was a fearsome sight to behold. A head taller than Ander's substantial height, with long, thin horns curling back from the crown of his head and eyes as black as pitch.

Even for all that, he was wearing a smile. "Aemiliana! What brings you to my corner of Underworld?"

"My son," Aemiliana said, her voice just shy of impolite. "One of your lords has him. What was his name again, Mab?"

"Enrique." Mab choked out the name, wishing not for the first time since entering the dark, obsidian chamber that Aemiliana had not insisted she come along. She would have been just as happy to wait back at the castle, or in the carriage.

"Enrique?" Hades blinked at her, his dark eyes a touch wider. Mab wished she could sink into the floor where he couldn't look at her. Or hide behind Aemiliana's skirts like a child. "Enrique," he repeated, frowning. "Enrique . . . Enrique . . . Oh!" Hades snapped his long brown fingers, the smile returning to split his face into something that could be almost friendly on someone who was not god of the dead. "You mean Orcus. Eryx, be a darling and summon Orcus. And tell him to bring Ander along."

The youth standing behind Hades, who Mab hadn't seen until that moment, bowed deeply and disappeared into the shadows to follow orders.

"Should we sit? I can have some refreshments brought." Hades motioned to a small sitting area that seemed to appear from the shadows, like it had been built from them.

"No, thank you. I just want my son."

"Oh, very well." Hades huffed, his shoulders sagging a little, face falling into a pout that looked very much like Ander's when Mab told him it was time to leave a party. "We get so few visitors from your land. I had hoped . . . Ah, but I understand. There are more important things."

"There are," Aemiliana agreed, and they fell into an awkward silence while they waited for Enrique and Ander to appear. Thankfully, they did a moment later, slipping out of the shadows.

Mab's heart was in her throat, threatening to choke her, at the sight of Ander before her again. He was even thinner now. And his eyes looked hollowed out from the inside, like a gourd on All Hallows Eve.

"What is the meaning of this?" Enrique asked, barely restrained fury lining his tone. He had Ander's hand in his, his nails digging into Ander's skin.

"It's time for you to come home, Ander," Aemiliana said, her eyes fixed on her son, not even bothering to dignify Enrique with a glance. "Mab and I would like you to come with us."

"He is home," Enrique said.

Ander gasped beside him, his shoulders hunching in a little further, and it took everything Mab had in her to stay rooted to the spot. To keep from striding across the black floors of Hades' receiving chamber and ripping Enrique's hand off Ander, maybe even from his body, if she could manage it.

"He came with me willingly. Didn't you, my princeling?" Enrique turned to coo at Ander, and Ander leaned into the softness of it like a flower seeking the sun, nodding absently.

"After you manipulated him," Mab spat, her voice shaking. Enrique's eyes narrowed on her, the glare so cutting, she was sure it had drawn blood.

"Excuse me?"

"You heard me." Mab lifted her chin.

"Mabbers . . . no. It wasn't like that at all." Ander shook his head, his brows creased.

"Whatever it was like," Aemiliana said, drawing Ander's eyes to her, "you're coming home with us, Ander. Now."

"You can't take him if—" Enrique started, all the poison and spite that Mab knew lived in his veins pouring out of him like water. He looked like he wanted to lash out at Aemiliana and Mab. To cut them the way he might one of the souls he tortured. But he was aware of where he was and of the eyes watching him. "He *wants* to be here."

"Be that as it may, Orcus, Ander will be leaving with his mother and sister today. If he wishes to return in a few months, I'm sure they will allow that. But until then, you must let him leave," Hades said. The friendly smile had gone, and he was all at once the ruler of the damned. Mab was glad he was not looking at her anymore. "Ander, please go with your mother."

Ander sucked in a breath, the sound too loud to Mab's ears. He moved onto his toes and pressed a lingering kiss to Enrique's jaw, his hands shaking, then whispered something in his ear. A promise, perhaps. One that Mab would die before she let him keep.

Then his sandals moved silently across the floor toward Mab and Aemiliana, and while he offered his mother a tentative smile, he would not meet Mab's eyes. That was fine. He could be angry with her all he liked. So long as he was safe.

Chapter 13
Ander

Helicon, Underworld

"I can't believe you would even *suggest* he would harm me, let alone kill me!"

"Andy, he *is* harming you. Look at yourself!"

The words were like a slap, and Ander turned on his heel to march away from the two most important women in his life, who were presently staring him down like judge and jury. The fact that Mab and his mother had waltzed into Hades' fortress to force him out had both humiliated and shamed him. What had they been thinking? What must Enrique be thinking now that this had happened before the god of death?

"I look at myself every day!" He whipped back around to shout at her. "It's taken everything I am to make myself look this good!"

"Oh, darling . . ." It was his mother. Her dark eyes filled with tears, and agony sounded in her voice, making him suddenly cease his pacing and actually look at her. Aemiliana came forward, her hands lifting to cup his cheeks as she forced him to meet her watery gaze. "Why have you let him strip you of your strength? Sweetheart, he's starved you into a shell of yourself."

Ander flinched and shook his head, pulling away from his mother's embrace. "Stop speaking about him like that," he growled. "He hasn't starved me—he's helped me find perfection."

Aemiliana's hand rose to cover her mouth, perhaps pushing back words she wished to say but had thought better of.

Ander had barely been able to look at either of them since they had pulled him out of Hades' fortress and into the waiting carriage. The ride from Acheron had been as silent as the truly dead. Neither his mother nor Mab deemed it appropriate to speak, and Ander had just sat silently, staring out the window, wondering when he'd ceased being able to make his own decisions about how to live his life.

"Andy, how can you say that?" Mab had come forward, her warm, brown face currently pinched with anger and hurt. "You never second-guessed your looks until that *rat bastard* came along—"

"Stop calling him that! I love him, Mab! Why can't you understand and accept that?"

"Because he's terrible for you!"

They were shouting at each other, standing only a few feet apart, their hands clutched into tight fists at their sides as they hurled words back and forth.

"You're just jealous!"

"Jealous? You honestly think that's what this is about?"

"Well, what else could it be about? You come to my mother, making up lies about some premonition, and have her drag me out of Enri's by the ear like some naughty school child! I'm not a child!"

"Then stop acting like one!" Mab spat.

He looked to his mother, ignoring Mab's words, making sure she was paying attention as he reasserted himself. "Neither of you get to tell me how to live my life."

"He's going to *kill* you, Ander! Not just kill you but burn you alive. I've seen it.

I've—"

"Stop!" He swept his hands before him, and with a blast of power, he forced her lips together for the moment, sealing up her words. "I won't hear any more of it. I don't know what you thought you saw, but Enri isn't like the others. He's not like the other males in my life who've hurt me. He loves me, and because he loves me, I want to be with him and I want to be who he wants me to be." He had never been enough for anyone, not as he was. Not for the people of Helicon, not for his grandfather, not for any of the other lovers in his past. But Enrique was staying. Enrique wanted him. And Ander would do anything he had to in order to keep him.

Shaking his head, Ander spun once more on his heel and headed for the door of his mother's chambers.

"Sweetheart, where are you going?" his mother called after him.

"To my rooms. And I wish to be left alone!"

Storming through the castle, Ander was soon enough at his personal quarters. As always, they were ready and waiting for whenever he chose to return home. It had been a while since he had last come to visit, Mab in tow.

Mab.

She'd always gone with him anywhere he went. His best friend. His companion. For over twenty years, they had been inseparable, and he hadn't wanted it any other way. Over the last six months, he had missed her terribly. He'd thought he would give almost anything to see her again and repair what had been cracked.

But Ander could see now that it wasn't just cracked. What rested between them had been broken. The thought that she would drag him from Enrique's side against his will and then make up lies about his intentions with Ander was more than he could take.

Once inside his chambers, he snapped his fingers, and several bottles of wine appeared on the table before him. Uncorking the first, he tipped it back and gulped deeply from its sweet depths.

As soon as he was able, he would return to Enrique's side. It would be a very long time before he allowed Mab Duchan to be in his presence again.

A fortnight had passed in which Ander spent most of his time drunk in his room. Occasionally, he allowed his mother to talk him into joining her and Mab for the evening meal. During this time, he simply sat staring at his plate, detesting the sight of everything they put before him.

He didn't have anything to say to either of them.

It was two weeks to the day when Enrique showed up. Had he gone to meet with Aemiliana, she would have denied him access, barring him from getting to Ander as he intended. However, too clever for that, Enrique made his way into the gardens and called up to Ander's window from the rose bushes.

Unable to believe his ears, Ander had hurried to his balcony and gazed down at his beloved face.

"Oh gods! What took you so long?'

"Miss me, princeling?" Enrique's face was upturned toward him, and the sunlight overhead shone down on him, highlighting his beauty and grace. He stole Ander's breath away all over again and made his heart thump wildly in his chest.

Enrique was like opium, muddling his senses and making him crave more. Ander wanted nothing as badly as he wanted the other man. Without thought, he snapped himself down into the gardens and threw himself into Enrique's arms. As they closed around him, strong and possessive, Ander released a pent-up breath he'd been holding since his mother hauled him out of Acheron.

"I missed you so, so much." Pulling back a little, he looked into Enrique's eyes. "I am so sorry for what happened! I can only imagine how that looked in front of Hades. I never wanted to be a cause for embarrassment."

Enrique's hands came up to cup his cheeks, and he pressed his thumbs to Ander's lips, silencing him. "Hush. Speak no more of it. You weren't to blame. Your mother and that so-called *friend* of yours are confused. They don't understand our love."

Ander shook his head in agreement. They didn't.

"If I could make it so they'd never be able to separate us again, would you do what it took?" Enrique asked.

"Of course I would." Ander sighed. He wanted nothing more than to be with Enrique.

From the pockets of his robe, Enrique pulled out two gold bands, which were shaped like arrows bent to form rings. Ander's breath hitched at the sight of them.

"Do you know what these are?"

"Yes." His voice was shaky, a strange feeling taking over him. One of breathless abandon but also heaviness. It was hard to breathe, like he was beneath a pool of water. "Aeternus rings . . . created by Venus."

Those who were joined by aeternus rings could not be separated. It bound them together and made it impossible for them to part. It was a show of absolute love and devotion. Once they were put on, the wearers could not remove them. It was said the only thing that could break the bond was the power of one of the original gods of Olympia.

Enrique slipped one onto his left hand, down to the base of the finger connected to his heart. He then held out the other to Ander.

"Ander Ruin, Crown Prince of Helicon, would you do me the honor of being bound to me eternally?"

Ander shivered, swallowing roughly. Nodding, he held out his hand and allowed Enrique to slip the ring over his finger. A shock of pure electricity ran through both of them, and a blast of light swirled around them before shooting straight into the sky.

Enrique drew him to his chest, crushing their lips against each other. Moaning at the fierceness of the kiss, Ander melted into him, letting himself be swept away by the force of nature that was this strong man.

When they parted, both were breathless. "Come, let's go let Her Majesty know you'll be coming home with me. Where you belong."

Ander shivered. "Yes, let's."

Hand in hand, they made their way into the castle. His mother was in the throne room speaking with one of the nobles. At the sight of Enrique and Ander together, she silenced the male and came forward.

"What is the meaning of this?" Her voice was hard, unyielding.

Clinging to Enrique's hand, Ander squared his shoulders. "Enri has come for me, and I am returning with him."

"Andy?" Mab's concerned voice sounded behind them. Hurried footsteps carried her to their side. In her hands, she carried a bouquet of his favorite flowers: orchids, ranunculus, and dahlias. "Don't do this."

He held out his hand, showing off the aeternus ring, which seemed to glow from its newly minted position on his finger. "Enri and I are bound. I *will* be going with him."

Aemiliana gasped, her fingers covering her mouth. "Oh, sweetheart."

"What?" Mab was looking between the both of them. "What is it?"

"There is nothing we can do, Mab. We have to let him go." There was a defeated tone in his mother's voice that Ander hated. But someday she would come to understand this was what he needed to do.

He and Enrique left the two of them standing there arm in arm, looking downcast and broken. It was a sight that tore at his heart and made him question what it was the two of them saw that made them hate his decision so greatly.

But he let Enrique take him back to Acheron. Let him lead him back to their shared chambers and peel the clothes off his body. Their lovemaking was both glorious and forceful. Equal parts wonder and pain. Enrique seemed determined to brand himself on every part of Ander's flesh so that he was no longer able to tell where he ended and Enrique began.

When at last it was over, and the two of them lay tangled in each other's arms, Enrique trailed kisses over the back of his neck, a hand pressed firmly to his chest, pinning him back against him.

"You are all mine now, Ander, and I will never let you go again," he murmured into Ander's ear, teeth biting at his throat to leave a mark there. "One day, we will rule Helicon together."

Chapter 14
Mab

Helicon, Underworld

Why would she lie about *that*? Why would Mab ever, *ever* lie about someone being burned alive? Especially Ander! Especially the first person she'd seen as family since . . .

Since . . .

A growl ripped from her chest, and Mab threw the bottle of perfume she'd had in her hands. The glass shattered against the wall, falling to the floor with a soft tinkling sound.

"How dare he," she hissed, grabbing another off the little vanity set in her rooms in Helicon, the anger making her voice and hands shake. "How dare he!"

Another crystalline bottle joined the first on the floor. She should likely feel bad about that. Should worry that she was being a bad guest to Queen Aemiliana, but Mab couldn't think past the haze of fury that ripped through her like a storm. By the time it had subsided enough for her to see clearly, glass littered the floor, her breathing had begun to come in hard pants, and her eyes burned with tears.

She scrubbed at them, hating how weak she was. She should have known better. Should have realized that what she had with Ander wouldn't—couldn't—last because nothing good in her life ever did. Not her family at the manor, not Edward, and not Ander. Eventually, everyone left her. And why shouldn't they? What did she really have to offer them, anyway?

That thought brought back the rage.

"Well, fine. If he doesn't want me, then fine! I'll just . . . I'll just go." Mab turned to haul her luggage from the wardrobe and begin stuffing it with the few things she'd brought with her. She'd been traveling light since Ander had left her behind, not seeing the point in frilly petticoats and grand dresses. Why bother? She wasn't going to any parties. Not without him.

"Go where?" a voice asked, making Mab's head whip to the door, where Queen Aemiliana was standing just inside of it, her arms crossed almost lazily over her chest. Those brown eyes swept down to the mess Mab had made of her room, but Aemeliana didn't say anything, she just pursed her lips and lifted her gaze back to Mab. "Where are you going, Mab?"

"He doesn't want me anymore. You heard him. He doesn't—" Mab sucked in a breath, forcing herself not to say the words that sat heavy on her tongue. *He doesn't need me.* She swallowed them down, letting their jagged edges cut her up so much from the inside, she was surprised when she didn't cough up blood. "I'll just go and get out of your hair. You've got more important things to do."

"Mab . . ." Aemiliana looked like she wanted to reach for Mab, to pull her into a hug so tight it might force all the broken parts of her back together.

Mab took a step back, making it clear she didn't want

that. She didn't. If she was going to be broken, she wanted to feel it. She didn't want anyone to try to fix her. Not again. Not *ever* again.

"You will always have a place here, among our people," Aemiliana said instead, but it sounded like she was trying to tell Mab something else. Like there were words under the words. Ander would have heard them, he was good at that, but Mab didn't.

"That's sweet, but I don't belong here. Not without—" Mab shook herself, turning back to her bag on the bed and stuffing the last of her things into it. There wasn't much left. A single dress and petticoat. Not that she'd need them where she was going, but it felt important not to leave anything of hers behind. Like Ander would track the scent of her later. He wouldn't. He'd never be coming back, he had made that very clear.

Aemiliana nodded as if she understood. She probably did. She was probably the only one in the world who understood the ripping, clawing feeling that was roaring through Mab's veins like a virus. "Shall I have someone create a portal for you?"

"No." Mab shook her head, zipping the bag. "I won't be going back to the mortal realm. Not this time." Likely not ever. There were too many reminders of Ander there, spread across the world like dandelion seeds in the wind. She wondered, half-dazed with pain, if they'd grow into flowers or if they'd rot in the soil like so many things did when the damp settled in back in Ireland. "I would appreciate a carriage though. To the nearest port, if you can?"

"Of course." Aemiliana bowed her head, her lips pursed like she wanted to say something else. Maybe ask Mab where she was going again. Maybe ask her to stay. Maybe promise that they'd find a way to get Ander back, no matter what. All of those things would be empty, they both knew that. Ander was never coming back. And Mab couldn't help but be furious with him for it. It was his fault, after all. He should have just listened to her, not called her a liar—believed her. But instead . . . Instead . . .

"I'm sorry I couldn't help him, Your Majesty. I tried," Mab whispered, the words only just loud enough for them both to hear.

"I know you did, sweetie." Aemiliana's voice was so quiet, Mab almost wasn't sure she'd heard it at all. And then she was gone, off to order a carriage for Mab, leaving Mab alone with the broken pieces of what her family had been.

She didn't belong in Helicon, not without Ander. She knew that better than anyone else. Without Ander, she didn't really belong anywhere. Well, except one place. The place where all good death omens went to disappear from the world.

Sophelia rose up from the sea, just as Mab remembered it. Beautiful, stoic, and terrifying all at once. Like Poseidon himself had erected it from the waters, and the sun had breathed life into it.

"Are you happy to be going home?" one of the other women on board the small boat asked. Mab hadn't bothered to learn their names. She wasn't going to Sophelia to make friends, after all. She was going there to disappear. To forget. To not *be* Mab anymore at all.

"Home," Mab repeated, hoping it would mean something when spoken from her own lips. But it didn't.

Sophelia wasn't home. The banshees and sirens who lived there weren't her family. Her family was gone.

The woman blinked at her, probably confused as to why Mab hadn't answered her question, but Mab didn't bother with it.

"Sister Mab," Sister Cassia said with what looked like a smug smile on her face when the boat docked. "It is good to see you again."

Although she had not spoken the words, Mab remembered what Cassia had said to her before she left. "They always come back." She'd been right, so very right, as if Cassia had looked into Mab's future and seen exactly what would happen to her in the coming months. What had been happening in her absence.

"Did you find what it was you were searching for?" Cassia asked the question carefully, casually, as they walked back up the pier to the main entrance into the monastery.

"No. I did not." Mab hoped the words didn't sound like the defeat that they were, but the little twitch of victory at the corner of Cassia's mouth dashed that hope.

"Most don't." Cassia nodded sagely. "Come, we still have your room made up."

Mab let Cassia lead her back to the cell she'd lived in during the months she'd been in Sophelia. She let Cassia remind her about the robes and the rules. No unnecessary talk. No drinking. No late nights. Just mindful meditation on the balance of the universe and how best their oracle abilities could fit into it. A problem they had yet to solve, as the elders of their kind, Cassia included, did not believe that they should interfere in the plans of the Fates.

She'd fit in this time, Mab vowed to herself. She'd follow all of the rules, and she'd be a good member of the order of the Fates.

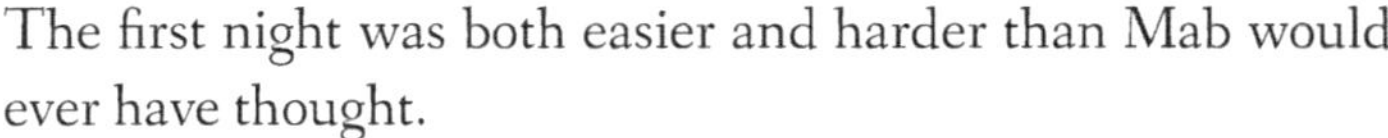

The first night was both easier and harder than Mab would ever have thought.

No one would so much as meet her gaze at dinner, as if perhaps they were afraid that whatever of the outside world she'd brought with her would infect them as well. And that was easier. Not having to explain what happened, what brought her back. The silence made it simple to disappear back into the fabric of Sophelia. To become just another thread on the loom of fate.

But when the darkness settled in around her, and she was left alone in her room, she found rather quickly that she couldn't sleep. That the darkness and the quiet rang with the echoes of everything that had been before.

And then she was sobbing into her pillow, her breaths hitching until she couldn't breathe at all around the ache in her chest. "I've failed him."

Chapter 15
Ander

Acheron, Underworld – August 1861

Ander should have felt elation. Returning with Enrique to Fortress Ploutos, bound together for all eternity; it was everything he had ever wanted. Love. Commitment. Forever.

But something was missing. Something had left him feeling hollowed out, and he knew it had everything to do with his mother and Mab. In the heat of the moment, his actions had seemed correct. He'd had two weeks to sit and think about what he wanted and where he wished to be.

Now that he had it, Ander wasn't so sure.

"Are you moping? *Again?*"

Ander jumped, turning from the window he had indeed been moping out of, and looked at Enrique, who bore a truly disgruntled look on his face. "I just . . . really miss my mom."

"*I miss my mom,*" Enrique echoed back at him in a petulant, childish tone.

"Don't be like that—" Ander's words were cut off as Enrique moved forward before he could blink and grabbed his chin tightly in his hand, jerking his head up. Ander winced and shrunk back a little at the ferocity in Enrique's eyes.

"Do. *Not*. Tell me what to do." His voice was low and threatening in a way that made Ander's blood run cold. He knew that his lover could be cruel and harsh—it was all in the job description. But he'd never had it aimed at him before.

"I—I wasn't. You were just being—"

"I was just being *what*?"

Ander knew well enough not to answer that. "Nothing," he whispered.

"That's right. I have given you everything you wanted, have I not? So do not be petulant with me. And stop moping around for your mother. You are not a child. You are a grown man and have made your choice. Don't make me regret mine."

As Enrique let go of his chin and turned away, Ander lifted his fingers to rub tenderly at the flesh he could tell was now bruised. His fingers trembled along his skin, and he dropped them into his lap so that he could squeeze his hands together, trying to make the trembling stop.

November 1861

It was as if a switch had been flipped in Enrique. Gone was the tender, loving male who had doted on him with affection and wonder. In his place was an ill-tempered being who found continuous fault with Ander. He was never tidy enough. Never put together enough. Too loud. Too energetic. Too needy.

Weak.

Foolish.

Embarrassing.

Ander didn't understand what had happened. Where was the man he loved? They were now together in a way no one could break apart. Why wasn't he happier? Wasn't this what he wanted?

"Do you want me to leave?!" Ander finally broke down one night, after Enrique had returned to their chambers and barely spoken two words to him. The inattention was the hardest. The way he could walk past Ander without even sparing him a glance, as if he were insignificant. A fly on the wall.

"What?" Enrique asked, barely paying attention. Too preoccupied with a scroll he had brought along with him.

"Do you want me to *leave*? You barely look at me anymore! You barely touch me! If you're second guessing our union, we can go and ask Hades to break the aeternus rings right now!" He was shouting, his throat raw from the emotion and force. Ander knew he was out of control, that Enrique wouldn't like this kind of crazed emotional display from him. But he couldn't take it anymore. "You can just be rid of me!"

Finally. *Finally*, Enrique was looking at him, the scroll forgotten as he faced Ander from across the room.

"Why would you suggest such a thing?" He seemed genuinely confused. Perhaps hurt?

"I don't think you love me anymore."

Enrique crossed the room, cupping his face in his hands and wiping the tears that had come unbidden from his eyes. "No, darling, don't speak like that. Of course I love you. I've just been busy. I know I haven't had much time for you lately, but it's only because Hades is pushing more responsibility onto me."

Ander bit at his lip, doubt swirling in his mind. It was more than just stress from his duties. Things had changed between them. Ander considered asking Hades for a breaking of the rings at least once a day.

"And you don't believe me . . ." Enrique sighed, his shoulders slumping. His face became crestfallen, eyes pained. "Do you not love me anymore, Ander? Is that what this is? I thought I had built a wonderful life for us, that one day we would rule Helicon together. But if it's not what you want . . ."

"No! Of course I love you." Ander lifted his hands to clutch onto Enrique's wrists. Although Ander had never wished to rule Helicon instead of his mother, nor had that changed. He just didn't have the heart or nerve to inform Enrique of that fact.

"Then is this life not enough for you? I've given you all that I can. I'm trying to work harder so that I can build a better place for us here. But if it's not—"

"No!" Ander rushed to cut him off, hating the way Enrique looked. As if he had failed Ander. "I'm just being foolish. I know you're stressed. I need to be more understanding." He leaned forward to press kisses to Enrique's lips, trying to show him how much he loved him. How much he cared.

Enrique's arms wrapped around him, pulling him into his chest. Wiping away Ander's doubt for the moment as he was reminded of how good they were together. Of the connection they had.

He was busy. That's all this was. Stress. Ander was his

safe place, where he could release it. He needed to stop holding that against him.

January 1862

Ander'd had a good day. He'd slipped out from under the ever-watchful eye of the servants and met Sora for drinks at a club that was attached to Earth. It was the first time in months that he'd been anywhere near the mortal realm, and he'd found it refreshing. To put on the formal suit and style his hair just so. Sora had looked ravishing in her corseted gown of light lavender. He'd told her so on more than one occasion.

She, in return, had laughed and squeezed Ander's hand, teasingly telling him to stop being such a flirt, even though she knew there was nothing behind it. It was simply nice to feel free and at ease. To see a smiling face across from him who delighted in his former charming self. Wanted to laugh at his ridiculous stories and gossip about the latest fashions and who was and wasn't pulling it off.

Snapping back to his quarters at Ploutos, Ander's head spun a little bit. He'd clearly had more of the brandy than he realized. But it felt good. The alcoholic buzz in his blood. The thrum of happiness and enjoyment still humming in his chest. He felt lighter than he had in a long time.

"Do you delight in making a mockery of me?" Enrique sat at the table before the fireplace, his elbows resting on his knees as he leaned forward. The firelight flickered over his features, casting half his face in shadows while highlighting the other half. It was chilling.

"What? I don't know what you mean." Ander's mind raced. Had he misbehaved in front of Hades? Spoken out of turn during the last formal dinner that was held here? He thought he had done everything that Enrique had wanted him to.

"I know about you and Sora." His voice was deep. Deadly.

Ander blinked, brow furrowing. "We had drinks," he said softly. "I'm a little tipsy, but I don't think anyone cared."

"Sorkis saw you."

Ander's heart shrunk a little. "Okay." There was a heavy boulder above him, ready to fall and crush him. Now he knew who was rolling it, but what was the actual weight of the stone?

This simple response angered Enrique further. His shoulders stiffened. His hands fisted. "He said you couldn't stop flirting with her. Laughing. Staring into each other's eyes. Holding hands. You may as well have just *fucked* her right there for all to see!"

Ander's breath hitched, and he took a step back. "That's not—"

"Not what?" Enrique was on his feet, coming toward him like an angry lion on the prowl. "Not what you were doing? Or not what you wanted me to find out about?"

Ander took another tentative step back. "I wasn't flirting. We were just chatting. And laughing over other patrons' clothes. I swear!"

Ander's head snapped sideways from the force of the blow that followed.

His ears rang, and his vision swam before his eyes, while

pain blossomed through his jaw. The slap had taken him so off guard, that Enrique had him pinned to the mattress of their bed before he was even aware of it, his heavy frame bearing down on him menacingly.

"Do I need to remind you of who you belong to, princeling?" Enrique snarled in his ear. "Me!" He spat the word, spraying Ander's face.

A whimper slipped from his lips that he was not proud of but could not control. "Get off me," he whispered.

"Get off you?" The snarl shredded all of Ander's courage. "Who do you think you are? Shaming me in front of my friends and confidants. My equals. While you are nothing but a misbegotten byproduct of your mother's indiscretion. An unwanted git that your grandfather couldn't stomach and wished to wipe from existence. You're not even a full muse, and your mother is too ashamed to admit what the rest of you is." Angry fingers began removing Ander's clothes, popping buttons and tearing the fabric.

Ander pushed at the broad expanse of Enrique's chest, trying to get away from his words. From the truth of himself that was being laid bare before him. What *was* he in comparison to the god of punishment?

"Please . . ."

"Please what?" Enrique growled, and then he spent the next hour proving to Ander just who he belonged to. Until Ander felt there was nothing left to him but what Enrique had possessed, broken, and left behind.

June 1862

The sun was shining in Acheron. But then, it always seemed to be shining. Heat drenched the land, adding to the fires that swelled below the earth. Somehow, even the smoke that billowed from the open mouth of Tartarus could not dim the scorching fingers of the large, yellow ball in the sky.

Ander wished that it would burn away every inch of his flesh. Scour the wounds—seen and unseen—that Enrique had left upon his body. If he stayed out here beneath it for long enough, perhaps it would. He closed his eyes against the brightness and begged for some reprieve.

It was the sound of a wheeled cart, clattering over the courtyard, that brought Ander's eyes open at last. It wasn't a typical cart but one that carried a large black cage. Inside, a bound ignis flailed, crashing himself against the bars in reckless disregard for his white and brown spotted wings.

Ander—unsure he was seeing things correctly—rose quickly to his feet and hurried over. Guards belonging to the ranks of Enrique's dungeon enforcement drove sticks of lightning between the bars, shocking the ignis until he cried out in agony and collapsed on the bottom of the cage. Only when he was unmoving did they open the cage and haul him out.

His head hung forward, body limp and unresponsive.

"What is going on?" Ander asked. This didn't seem right. In fact, it felt truly wrong. Apprehension and horror rolled through him.

The guards ignored him and dragged the ignis inside.

Ander faltered. If this was Enrique's doing, and he didn't want Ander's interference, there would be hell to pay. If this was Hades' business, Ander had no place in it.

But he couldn't seem to help himself.

He followed them down the halls and to the lower level where the dungeons were located. Here was Enrique's domain, where he punished the dead who had lived terrible lives.

The guards dragged the ignis into an inner chamber, one that glowed with the light of lava and flames. When he tried to step through the door, two of the guards blocked his path.

"No, let him come in," Enrique's voice called from inside.

When the guards moved out of the way, Ander was able to go into the room. It was carved out of black pumice stone. Handcrafted from lava to be the perfect torture chamber. A large stone slab stood erect on one side of the room, chain cuffs attached at the top corners. A stone table with sharp spikes along its surface sat on the other. In the middle of the room, hanging by his wrists from chains in the ceiling, was the ignis, his ankles also chained to the floor.

"Enri?" Ander whispered. "What is this?" The very sight of it made his skin crawl. The ignis were eternal beings who had been crafted as perfect warriors. Formed in the forges of Prometheus' primordial flame, they upheld the safety and protection of humans in the mortal realm.

They were what kept the beings of Underworld from rampaging through the human world. They were why humans believed in angels.

"This . . . is my play toy." The smirk on his face was dark and unyielding. To make his point, Enrique lifted a cat-o'-nine-tails from a rack along the wall and brought it down upon the chest of the ignis. The male came alive, body arching as he growled in pain. His large wings spread out, showing off their glorious beauty. Flapping them, he attempted to pull himself free of the chains, to no avail.

Enrique laughed watching him. "Futile efforts, soldier. These bindings were made to hold stronger than you."

"You will pay for this, Orcus," the ignis spat.

Enrique's only response was to bring the whip down on his flesh once more, shredding his chest with fine lines of bright red, which dripped with blood.

"Enri!" Ander gasped. "What are you doing?"

"Experimenting. I want to see what he can take."

"This is . . ." His mind told him to stop. That standing up to Enrique had never gotten him anywhere before. He would only pay for it later. But his heart told him that he had to. That he wouldn't be able to sleep at night if he didn't try and step between Enrique and the bound male. "This isn't right!"

Ander rushed to get between the next sting of the whip, throwing up a magical shield to block both of them from harm. Enrique did not look amused, but he also did not look furious. He eyed Ander as if he were a child attempting to stand up to an elephant.

"Get out of the way."

"No. You can't simply hurt him to see what will happen."

"Don't fret. Prometheus built the ignis as veritable walking shells. They were made for one purpose and one purpose only. If they die doing it, so be it. He cared so little about them, he didn't even bother to give them emotions. Their only thoughts are of their mission."

"That doesn't mean you can torture him! He feels pain."

Enrique's eyes narrowed. "Fine. I won't torture him." Ander's shoulders relaxed. "You will."

"What?" Shaking his head, Ander stepped away from them. "No, I will not."

"No?" Enrique closed the distance between them, holding out the whip. "Would you prefer that it were Mab down here instead of him?"

Ander gasped, his stomach knotting and heart constricting. "You wouldn't." His voice was soft, disbelieving.

"Wouldn't I?"

Ander swallowed the bile that threatened to spill into his mouth. He was not a violent man, and this . . . this was more than he had ever done before.

"I can't."

Enrique's brow shot up. "It's either the ignis, or it's the banshee. Either way, I am testing someone's limits today."

With a shaking hand, Ander reached out to take the whip.

"No, on second thought . . . use the knife."

Ander fled outside, making it only to the bottom of the fortress steps before he was leaning over with his hands braced on his knees and spewing every last bit of what was in his stomach. His skin crawled. Everything felt dirty, from his fingertips to the recesses of his mind. His ears echoed with the cries of pain that had been rung out of the creature in the dungeons.

Looking down at his feet, Ander saw that they were red with blood.

Leaning over once more, he gagged, stomach clenching forcefully even though there was nothing left to bring up.

He couldn't stay here any longer. It was one thing to leave himself in the hands of this monster, but to witness and be forced to partake in his torture was the end. Ander would rather die than be trapped here one second longer.

Snapping his fingers, he teleported himself to Helicon.

Or at least he tried. Halfway through the move, he felt the pull of the ring snap into place and yank him back to Acheron. He hit the ground hard, not expecting the violent recoil or sudden release. Rolling over the ground, he finally came to a stop.

"I will not stay here!"

Ander snapped again, and again, and again. Each time, the ring on his left hand would pull him back, slamming his body into the ground. No amount of magic would pull the ring from his finger. It was doing exactly what it was supposed to do: keep the two of them from being separated when one did not agree to it.

Screaming in defeat, Ander pounded on the ground until his hands were bloody and numb, the desperation of his situation truly overtaking him. He was trapped here. Unable to leave unless Enrique agreed. Which was something he was never going to do.

With one last, desperate hope, Ander lifted his hand to his head and plucked from his temple a small iridescent drop that grew into a bubble. Into it he poured his thoughts, his despair, his regret, and his need. Adding just a dash of the horrors of his life, he sealed the thought bubble so that it would open to no one but Mab.

"Find her," he whispered to the bubble, then sent it off.

If it didn't work, or she didn't come, Ander didn't know what he would do.

Perhaps it was too late and she had already cast him off for all he had said and done.

Rubbing his hands over his face roughly, Ander screamed into his palms, releasing a blast of magic to propel the thought bubble on, and quickly. This was no longer just about him. It was about Enrique too, who he was quickly learning was a despicable mad man.

Chapter 16
Mab

Mab didn't know why she'd thought she could make herself fit in with the others of her kind in Sophelia. She should have known better. She was too loud. Too bright. Too *much*. And that became increasingly evident by the day. Every hour brought some new instance of those around her looking at her like she was the odd one out. The strange thing that had spent too long among the humans and a muse to understand their need of silence and solitude.

Surprisingly, it wasn't so much the lack of conversation that got to Mab in the end. It was the silent acceptance. The quiet bowing of the head. The lack of questions asked. That when Cassia gave an order, it was followed, considered to be what was best for all of them, and no one once asked why.

It all came to a head one day some months later when one of the sirens—a young woman named Delila who had been born in the mortal realm, as Mab was, but had suffered none of the horrors that Mab had seen—fainted during their evening meal. Those around her watched her tumble to the floor, her back thumping hard against the tiles, before turning back to their meal as if nothing at all had happened.

Mab half-rose from her seat but was stopped by Ronen, who laid her own tan hand on Mab's, and when Mab looked to her, shook her head. Her legs trembled as she lowered herself back to the bench, wondering if Delila was sick or dying. She seemed so young—although they all did when Mab really thought about it, ageless beings who had stopped maturing past their mid- to late-twenties.

When Mab looked back, Cassia was beside Delila, kneeling on the hard floor, brushing her long blond hair back from her pale face. Delila's eyes were open, staring unseeing up at the ceiling, and her lips were moving too quickly for Mab to make out the words. It took a small infinity for Delila to come back to herself, but once she had, Cassia helped her to her feet and escorted her from the room.

A soft grip on her wrist, a reminder and an order all in one, did not stop Mab from following. She was a short clip behind them, close enough to hear them but far enough away that they wouldn't notice her there, hopefully.

"But she'll die if I don't," Delila said, her voice soft, pleading, and louder than Mab thought she'd ever heard it. There was a note of desperation there that Cassia insisted on beating out of them with a rigorous schedule and meditation.

Cassia shook her head, a hard look on her features that Mab could only just make out from the place where she'd tucked herself behind a pillar. "It is not our place to interfere."

She'd said that before to Mab, when Mab had first returned and told Cassia of what might happen to Ander.

That it wasn't their place to interfere. That they were just recorders of the prophecies, not enactors of change. And Mab had accepted it then because it made things easier. It made it simpler to think that her failure to save Ander was out of her hands. That there was nothing she could have done, even if she'd stayed. But something turned in her stomach at the jerk of Delila's body, the words landing like a blow.

"I love her, Cassia. You must understand. I can't just leave her to that fate." Delila's voice shook with some emotion that Mab couldn't see, as she was turned away from her. "I love her."

"And that is why our kind do not leave Sophelia," Cassia said, her tone hardened by her years of ruling the women of the island. "We cannot form attachments to the outside world. It only makes things harder."

Delila let out a soft whimper, and Cassia sighed, her shoulders sinking a little before she moved to take the younger woman's hands, giving them a firm squeeze and pulling her in close. It was a kind gesture. Motherly, in its way. But there was nothing maternal in the look on Cassia's face. There never had been. Not as long as Mab had known her.

"And what if you save her? What then? Who will die in her place? How will that upset the fabric of fate?" Cassia asked when she pulled away to look Delila in the eyes. "Are you willing to make that sacrifice for your beloved? To bring down the entire tapestry of the grand design?"

"I have to try." Delila's voice had grown stronger, her chin lifted and shoulders straightened in her resolve. "I have to—"

"It won't work." Cassia's expression had gone cold, hard, losing any trace of the kindness it had held a moment ago.

Her eyes flicked over Delila's shoulder, and Mab knew she'd been spotted, but she was rooted to the spot. Eavesdropping wasn't strictly forbidden, but it was rude. It didn't matter. Mab couldn't move.

"Wh-what?" Delila's shoulders had begun to shake again, the word garbled up by a sob.

"It won't work. Whatever you try, however long you're able to waylay her death, it won't work. In the end, death will come for her. The world's scales will always rebalance themselves. That is the rule of the Fates, and we do not go against the Fates." Cassia may have been speaking to Delila, but her eyes were narrowed on Mab. A cold hard truth settled like a chill into Mab's bones. "Is that what you want, Delila? To spend a few days more with her, trying everything you can to save her, only to lose her in the end? Wouldn't that pain be worse than leaving it as it is, your goodbyes already said? Isn't that a kindness."

Delila let out a soft, strangled noise, but she nodded quickly in agreement.

"Good. Now, return to your supper. I'll be in in a moment." Cassia spared the girl a smile but didn't move as Delila disappeared back into the dining hall, her sandaled feet moving perhaps a little too quickly against the stone path. Once she was gone, it was just Cassia and Mab in the courtyard, the reality of all that had been said stretched between them. "You're planning to leave us again, aren't you?"

"Yes." Mab stepped from behind the pillar to meet Cassia's angry gaze head-on. What would it matter? She didn't fit here in Sophelia. Why should she stay and pretend? Why should she stay and let Ander die?

"Is this about the premonition you had of the muse?"

It wasn't wholly about that, Cassia had to know. Mab

had felt her eyes on her the last several months. Watching. Waiting. Reminding and reprimanding in turn when Mab stepped out of line. "Not entirely."

"You do not agree with what I told Delila?"

"I don't." Mab shook her head, the hood of her robe falling into her eyes, nearly blocking Cassia from view. "Why should we have visions of the future, of people dying, if not to change it? Wouldn't that be too cruel, even for the Fates?"

Cassia tilted her head, a frown lining the delicate skin around her mouth. "You'll learn in time that I'm right," she said, her voice almost pitying. "That no matter what you do, you can't change fate."

Mab sucked in a breath, raising her chin. "Maybe I will. But I have to try."

There was a nod, some of Cassia's dark hair falling into her face, and a resigned expression replaced the frown. "When you do, you will no longer be welcome here. Can you accept that? For some man?"

"He's not just some man." Mab snorted, rolling her eyes. She'd never heard Ander described that way before, and she doubted she ever would again. "He's my brother."

"Then you've made your choice." Cassia bowed her head in acceptance. "We will miss you, Sister Mab."

"No, you won't." Mab laughed and turned on her heel to head back to her cell and gather up her things. She wouldn't wait another moment. Wouldn't leave Ander with that monster a second longer. Not if she could help it.

"Oh, Andy, you absolutely brilliant imbecile, I should never have left you," Mab said, the bubble resting in her hand. She knew it was from him, but she hadn't let it pop yet, almost afraid of all that it would contain.

Still, she needed to know how bad it was, so she poked her finger toward the center of the bubble, ignoring the way those around her on the boat watched with strange looks. By the time the vision cleared, she was choking back sobs, her eyes burning and her breath hitching.

"Miss?" the ferryman asked, his voice sounding like it was coming through water as Mab clung to the railing of the boat. "Are you all right, miss?"

"I'm going to fucking kill that bastard," Mab managed to choke out through the lingering sobs. Those around her took a step back, but Mab hardly noticed, as she was already planning all of the things that she could do to end the god of punishment.

Olympia, Underworld

How did one kill a god? She would not be able to do it herself, Mab realized irritably. For all that she was immortal, she wasn't strong enough, nor did she possess any actual magic. So, the first order of business once she reached land was to contact Aemiliana and set up a meeting with Hades.

Except Aemiliana had instructed her to seek out Indra instead, and had written her a letter to gain her an audience just in case. That's how Mab found herself being led down one of the long, brightly lit halls of Olympia into a receiving room with enough gilding on the walls to fund the British army for decades.

"And to what do I owe the pleasure, daughter of Sophelia?" a tall man asked from the raised dais, where he was lounging across a velvet chaise, his too-long legs flopped over the arm and his blond head cushioned in the lap of a sprite.

Mab bit down on the tip of her tongue to keep from spitting that she wasn't a daughter of Sophelia. "I'm here about Ander Ruin. Queen Aemiliana said you could help."

Indra sat up quickly, his pale eyes going wide with something she didn't think she was supposed to see before he rose to his full height to look down on her further. "Help with what, exactly?"

"Killing the god of punishment and rescuing my brother." Mab probably should have bowed and groveled and begged like some peasant. Indra was the king of the gods after all. But fury burned in her veins, and her heart was hammering against her chest, whispering, *Too late. Too late. What if you're too late?* and she couldn't think past any of it.

"Leave us," Indra said to the girl, then waited till they were alone before his eyes narrowed for a moment on Mab. "Your brother?"

"Yes." She'd never called him that out loud, not before speaking with Cassia a few days ago. Never admitted, really, what he was to her even to herself. But Ander was her brother. Her family. The only thing she had left. And she was going to bring him home if it was the last thing she did.

"Explain."

She did. She told him about the premonition, and the call for help, and the rings that Enrique had used to bind them together. When she was finished with her story, her throat was dry, and her breath was threatening to hitch again. But Mab didn't have time for that, not with Ander's life on the line, so she swallowed it all down.

"Will you help me or not? Because if it's not, then I've got to go and find someone else," Mab said, lacking all the respect she should show him. She wasn't trying to be rude, but she really didn't have the time or the patience to play politics.

"Daughter of—" Indra stopped himself. His lips pursed for a moment, and then he smiled, the expression all teeth and no joy. "Sister of Ruin, of course I'll help you. Let me just grab my cloak. Then we'll go find Juno, I'm sure she'll wish to join in on the excursion."

"Great," Mab squeaked. Relief washed over her so sharp and heavy, it nearly made her knees buckle, but she nodded and waited for Indra to go and ready himself.

Chapter 17
Ander

Acheron, Underworld   August 1862

Ander hated that he had woken up. Each new morning welcomed him back into the same hell he had left the night before.

He hated that he could feel Enrique's arm thrown over his body, holding him firm against his chest. His form curled around him; another prison holding him captive. No escape. There was no escaping this nightmare he had walked himself willingly into. Perhaps this was his punishment for Estelle. For abandoning Mab. For ever daring to be born.

This was where the unloveables went to die.

The desperate need to leave, to be out from under the weight of his eternal burden, rose up inside him. Like there were a million anxious beetles scurrying beneath the surface of his skin, burrowing into his bones, eating up his insides. Feeding a sickness that never left the pit of his stomach.

Mab had never come.

Mab had never come, so Ander resigned himself to living out this life of tiny, daily horrors.

A set of lips pressed against the back of his neck, and Ander squeezed his eyes shut as the sickness swelled up once more.

"Good morning, princeling," Enrique whispered into his ear.

Ander remained silent, keeping his eyes shut. If he appeared to be sleeping, perhaps Enrique would roll out of bed and leave him alone. The Fates were finally on his side: when he received no response, Enrique removed his arm from around Ander and climbed from the bed.

Laying there, Ander fought to keep his breathing even, not allowing his dread to overtake him and speed it up. When at last Enrique had left their chambers, he was able to release a breath of relief and finally relax. But not in the bed. He hated the bed. Hated everything that he was forced to share with Enrique.

Ander crawled out from under the covers and moved to the gilded tub in the dressing chamber off the side of the room. With a wave of his hand, he filled the tub with steaming water and submerged himself in its scalding depths.

Every morning, he scrubbed his flesh, removing every last trace of Enrique. Once he was finished, he dried off and applied lilac scented oils—Enrique hated it. It was Ander's one act of rebellion each day.

When he was dressed in one of the outfits Enrique had bought him and had styled his hair in the manner Enrique approved of, Ander went in search of someone—anyone—to distract himself.

There was an eerie quiet to the fortress today. Servants hurried past him with their heads down, barely taking the time to curtsy in greeting. At last, he stopped someone, startling the female so that she squeaked in surprise.

"What can I do for you, Your Highness?"

That title. It had kept him from making friends with anyone who lived here.

"What is going on today? Everyone seems near frantic."

The servant took a moment to reply. "A new boat of souls arrived today."

"Oh."

Taking his simple response to mean he was finished, the servant continued past him, heading to wherever she'd been on her way to when he stopped her.

New souls had arrived. Ander knew what that meant. It meant that Hades and Enrique would be busy all day completing intake. Once Hades had judged each soul for where they belonged, Enrique and Sophocles would take those who were meant for his hellish dungeon.

Ander had the entire day to himself.

He could have gone anywhere. Into the gardens. Escaped into the city. Or gone back to bed to finally sleep peacefully and freely. Instead, his feet carried him down the stone stairwell into Enrique's dungeons. He would not be here until much later. The processing of the souls always took the brunt of the day.

It would be hours before Enrique returned to the depths of his pumice-lined torture chambers.

Had someone asked him, Ander wouldn't have had an explanation for why he went where he did. Only that something inside him drew him to the cell that held the ignis.

The soldier was naked except for a scrap of leather wrapped around his waist like a loincloth. His once muscular body seemed frail and starved. His hair was lanky with filth, and his body was covered in bruises, cuts, and scars. The most devastating sight, however, were the jagged bones protruding from his back where his beautiful, powerful wings had been shorn from his body.

Ander audibly gasped when he saw it, his hand flying to his mouth as bile rose up in his throat. Who would de-wing a bird of prey and expect it to survive? The beetles were beneath his skin once more, crawling with a ferocity that threatened to carry him away.

The ignis lifted his head, gazing at him through the limp strands of his hair. "What do you want, muse?" His voice rasped with the roughened damage of screaming.

"I don't know," Ander said honestly. He didn't know why he was down here, except that perhaps a part of him had needed to see what had become of the creature in the dungeons.

It was worse than he had imagined. So much worse. On top of his disgust was a mounting anger filling his blood with fury that seemed to outweigh any and all of his better sense.

"Enough," Ander whispered. And it was enough. Enough of these games that Enrique was playing. Enough of his unyielding rule over others whose lives he had no right to. No true say in.

Standing back, Ander raised his hand toward the cage.

"What are you doing?" the ignis asked.

"Getting you the *hell* out of here." He didn't care what happened to him. Not anymore. Let Enrique beat him. Let him tell Hades he'd set one of his prisoners free. Let him kill him. None of it mattered anymore.

"What?"

"Getting. You. Out." Ander focused on the lock of the cell and sent a blast of power toward it. At first, it only rattled, flashing with a sign of the magic Enrique had used to seal it shut.

"It's pointless," the ignis said. "Please . . . just set me free."

"That's what I'm trying to do." Ander focused another heavy blast of magic at the door. This time it creaked but did not open.

"No. Kill me." The ignis crawled forward, his chains rattling. Grasping onto the bars nearest to him, he gazed up at Ander imploringly.

"What?" Ander stared in shock. "I won't kill you!" Another wave of magic burst against the lock.

"Please, it's the only way. Do it before they hear what you're doing and come down."

"No, this will work!"

"Have mercy on me! I need this to end."

Ander refused to give up. Refused to take the easy way out. "No!" This time, as the magic landed with more force and power behind it, the door flew off the hinges and landed on the floor with a loud crash. "I did it!" Hurrying into the prison cell, Ander reached for the chains around the ignis, beginning to work on releasing those as well. "See, I told you I would get you out."

"There's no time!" He turned to grab Ander's wrist, holding onto it surprisingly tight for someone in as weakened a state as he was. "They're coming. Can't you hear them?"

Ander paused. He could indeed hear shouting from above. "I can do this. I can snap us outside at least, and you can make a run for it." His heart was pounding in his ears as he broke the chains off the other male.

"*Please.* They're going to stop us, and I will remain in

this cell until he finally decides to end it. I can't take anymore."

"I can get you—"

"I don't want to live! Without my wings—" He broke down then into ragged sobs.

The shouting from above was growing louder, and Ander could hear thundering footsteps. Swallowing roughly, his heart almost drowned out the sound of his own voice as he asked, "What is your name?"

The ignis met his eyes. "Ikari."

"It's nice to meet you, Ikari. I am Ander." Somehow his voice remained steady, even though his hands shook as he reached out to pull Ikari into his arms, holding him tenderly against his chest. "I'll make it swift and peaceful."

"Thank you." It came out in a sigh of relief.

Pressing his hands against Ikari's back, Ander used his magic to send a wave of heat through his body that would both relax him and tell his body to shut down. He felt Ikari settle into him in peace, just as the guards—and Enrique— came upon them in the dungeons.

"What have you done?!"

Ander met Enrique's eyes with defiance, a wash of resilience filling him. He may not be able to fight him physically, but he could fight by other means. If Enrique killed him, then so be it, but he was done cowering in the corner. "I released one of us from your hell."

Enrique was upon him quickly, hauling him to his feet. Ander wanted to continue holding on to Ikari, but he wasn't strong enough. A cry of sorrow slipped from him as Ikari's body dropped gracelessly to the floor. "You could have some respect for him now at least!"

"Silence!" Enri snapped. "You had no right to do what you've done." He pulled him up the stairs of the dungeon, not caring when Ander tripped or if he was struggling to keep up.

In one last desperate act, Ander reached behind him and used his magic to snatch one of the white feathers from Ikari's cage. Needing to keep some part of the ignis with him.

Ander could only laugh bitterly at Enrique's words. "No right? No *right*? You have no right!"

As they reached the main level of the fortress, Ander wrenched his arm free of Enrique. Panting from his efforts, he rolled his shoulders and stood up straighter.

"Who do you think you are, little princeling?"

"No longer your possession."

Enrique growled darkly at this, then slapped him harshly across the face.

His head swung to the side, and his ears rang, but Ander only grinned at him, wiping the blood from his lips. "Is that the best that you've got?"

It was crazy to provoke him, but Ander wanted a resolution. However this ended, he didn't care, so long as it ended.

Enrique launched himself at Ander, grabbing him around the throat. He slammed him up against the brick wall and began to squeeze, cutting off his air. Clawing at his wrists, Ander kicked out at Enrique's shins and rocked himself against him in an attempt to free himself.

His vision was beginning to darken around the edges as blood and air fought to reach his brain. Clamping his hands tightly around Enrique's wrists, he used his magic to begin burning the flesh off of his hands. Maybe it would not be permanent—Enrique was a god after all—but it would hurt.

Howling, Enrique pulled back, shaking his hands out. Gasping for breath, Ander rubbed at his throat. With the brief moment of distraction, he turned and ran for the main door.

His escape did not last, and soon, Enrique was on top of him. His head slammed into the stone floor and fists pummeled him until the darkness threatened to overtake him.

It was a shot of lightning that separated them, sending Enrique skidding across the floor and into one of the opposite walls. Sparks sizzled on Ander's clothes, and he had to beat out the small flames that threatened to become more.

"How dare you! Stay out of this!" Enrique screamed, a sword materializing in his hand.

"How dare *I*?" a scandalized voice roared. "Who do *you* think you are to speak to me in such a manner?"

Pushing himself up off the floor a little, Ander sobbed at the sight of King Indra, his mother, and Mab.

Mab.

She had come for him.

Chapter 18
Mab

Acheron, Underworld

Mab stumbled across the floor, the hard soles of her boots skidding but not slowing her down. Nothing could slow her down. He was in reach. He was so close. He was right there in front of her. And she needed to get to him. She needed to pull him into her arms again, and hold him close, and feel his pounding heart against her own ribs as it screamed, *I'm alive. I'm alive. I'm alive.*

"You came for me," Ander gasped, his voice disbelieving and a little strangled from whatever torment Enrique had inflicted upon him.

"I did." Mab's arms wrapped around him so tightly, she was worried she might break something, but she couldn't seem to stop herself. She had to hold him. She had to know he was there. She needed to feel every shuddering breath. "I should have been here sooner. I'm so sorry, Andy. I should have come sooner. I shouldn't have left you with him for so long. I should have come sooner. Had I known. Had I known. Had I known." She was muttering, the words only half making sense even to herself, but every one of them was pressed into his skin, and nothing else mattered. Not the battle beyond them as Indra subdued Enrique. Not that monster's wails of how unfair, and how dare, and that Ander had asked for this, wanted it. None of it mattered. Because her Ander, her brother, was in her arms, and she was never letting go. Not again.

Someone was sobbing, their breaths broken and hitched. It might have been Ander. It might have been Mab. It was probably both of them. But she couldn't bring herself to care about what it might look like to everyone else there. How weak she might seem. What was weakness and vulnerability to the fact that she'd nearly lost the most important person in her world? Nothing.

"I'm here. I'm here. I'm here. I would have been here sooner. I would have stopped this if I'd known. I'm so sorry Andy. I'm so—"

Ander lifted his head from her shoulder, his trembling hands holding her cheeks—they were so thin and pale, it made something in her chest scream. "This isn't your fault, Mab."

And then she was crying harder than she ever had before, burying her face in his shoulder and clinging to him so hard she could hear the seams of his clothing creaking. "I would have come sooner. I would have." She hiccupped, the feeling of it jarring her body. "I was in Sophelia. We can't get messages there."

Ander nodded against the wet spot she could feel forming on her own shoulder. He was hurting. He was half starved. His eyes were darker, more haunted. But he was alive—alive, alive, alive, she still wasn't sure that she wasn't dreaming—and the rest could be sorted out later.

Someone cleared their throat behind Mab, and she

jerked back to cut a glare at whoever would dare disturb them, only to find Indra's bright blue gaze fixed on the pair. He offered her a triumphant smirk before saying, "Apologies. We need to get the bond taken care of." He nodded to Ander's left hand.

"Oh. Oh, of course," Mab said, pulling back only just enough to help Ander to his feet. As she made to take a step back from Ander so that Indra could do whatever he needed to, she threaded their fingers together, giving his hand a squeeze. "I'm not going anywhere, Andy," she promised, and she meant it. Not again. Not ever again.

"Me either, Mabbers." He returned the squeeze, his thumb brushing over her knuckles, then he turned to nod at Indra. "All right. Let's get this over with."

"Don't you dare! He's mine! He'll always *be* mine!" Enrique shouted from where two of Indra's men had forced him to his knees, his face a blotchy red patchwork in his fury. But his eyes were fixed on Ander like he was something to be had and owned. A possession.

"I will *never* be yours, Enrique," Ander shot back, a quiet strength in his words that Mab hadn't heard since the day she came home to find Enrique had inserted himself into their lives. Then he held out his hand to Indra, the ring glinting in the low light. "Do it."

There was a flash, the bolt of lightning streaking so brightly it nearly blinded. Mab raised her hand to shield her eyes, and a moment later, the ring clattered to the floor with a sound that echoed freedom and relief. Ander seemed to take the first real breath he'd taken since Mab had entered the room.

"No!" Enrique screamed, scrambling to get at them again. His rage cut through the two lesser gods Indra had assigned to hold him. And then he was on his feet and running toward them with a sword in hand, hurried steps eating up the ground between himself and Ander. Mab shifted quickly, putting herself in between them, blocking Ander from any further harm.

"Enough, Orcus!" a new voice boomed, all authority and power.

Enrique stopped before Hades, his eyes going almost comically wide in his face. Mab would have laughed at it in any other situation. She was sure Ander would have joined her. But not now. Not when Enrique had caused so much hurt and nearly broken the person Mab loved the most.

"He gave himself to me," Enrique argued, voice soft as he lowered his head. "I did nothing wrong."

"Indra?" Hades asked, turning to his brother. "What is the meaning of this?"

Mab opened her mouth to say something—what, she wasn't sure. Aemiliana caught her gaze and shook her head. With pursed lips, Mab pulled Ander in close again and listened to Indra tell Hades everything that had happened. He made quick work of it, she was surprised to find, and didn't seem half as infuriated by what had happened as she was. But then, she supposed that getting emotional at a time like this wouldn't really serve any of them, and what she needed to be focused on was getting Ander away from Acheron and back home. Back to the warmth and safety of his mother's kingdom, where the healing could really begin.

Ander shifted in her arms, letting out a soft sob as he pulled a downy white feather from somewhere on his person. Stroking it reverently between long fingers, he murmured, "And Ikari."

"What?" Indra asked, his brows drawn as he fixed his pale gaze on them.

"An ignis," Ander said, pulling his head from where it

had been buried against Mab's shoulder. "He captured one. Tort—" He choked on the word. "Tortured it, *him*. Tortured him. Tore off his wings. His name was Ikari, and he's dead because of what Orcus did to him."

"I see," Hades said when Ander had finished speaking. He turned back to Enrique, who had been bound by Indra's men again, his brows raised. "Do you have anything to say for yourself?"

"He came . . . He came willingly." Enrique's voice was faint, defeated already, pitiful, pathetic. Mab wanted to spit at his feet. Tell him that he had no excuse to sound like that after everything he'd done to Ander. After all the hurt he'd caused. Another shake of the head from Aemiliana silenced her.

"For your crimes against the muses," Hades said, lifting his chin up higher so he could look down his nose at Enrique, "you are sentenced to a hundred years of empathy. For every lash of your whip, every slice of your knife against one of the damned you torment, you'll feel it tenfold."

"Yes, Your—"

"*What?!*" Mab roared before anyone could stop her. Someone gripped her forearm, the hold almost hard enough to bruise. "That's not enough! He should be executed! He should—"

"Mab," Aemiliana cut, moving in front of her to level her with a serious look, dark eyes narrowed. "That is the punishment Hades sees fit for his crimes. We have no place in this decision."

"You can't—You don't know what he *did*! He doesn't deserve to—"

"Let's just go home, Mabbers," Ander whispered, his nails digging into her arm, leaving behind crescent shaped marks. "Please, Mabbers, I just want to go home."

He gave her arm a weak tug, and she let out a long breath. "All right, Andy. Let's go home."

Helicon, Underworld

The halls of Helicon felt different than they had before, more somber, heavy with the weight of all that had happened since the last time Mab had been there. She'd been so angry. Furious with Ander and everything that he'd said. Upset with herself for having failed him. Now, all she felt was impossibly tired and drained. Like every bit of fury had been sucked out of her.

They didn't speak—not that there was much to say, in Mab's mind—just headed to Ander's quarters and shut the door behind them.

"I need a bath," Ander said, his shoulders sagging. "And new clothes."

Mab nodded, already making her way toward the bathroom with his hand still clutched tightly in her own. "I'll sit with you."

"You really don't have to."

"I want to." Mab gave his hand another squeeze and pushed the door to the bathroom open with her hip. "I'm not letting you out of my sight for at least the next decade," she joked, but there was truth under it. So much truth. Because she couldn't let him become the plaything for someone else like Enrique. She couldn't sit back and watch him wither away under the hate and darkness of another.

Not again. He was too precious to her. Too dear. "I'm afraid you're stuck with me."

Ander looked up suddenly, his eyes so wide they almost ate up his whole face for how thin he'd become over the last couple of years. "You promise?"

"Andy." She said the name on a breath, leaning in to press her forehead to his so that she could make sure his gaze wouldn't shift away from her own. "You wouldn't be able to get rid of me now if you tried. We're family."

A soft, choked, bitten-off sob left Ander, then he was crumpling against her again, and Mab had just enough time to gather him into her arms and lower them both carefully to the cold marble floor of the bathroom. "Shhh. Shhh. It's okay. It's all going to be okay now," she soothed, stroking her hand through his hair, down his back, pulling him closer still when he clung to her like a drowning man. "Come on. Let's get you into the tub. I'll even wash your hair for you."

He nodded, the motion jerky, bumping almost too hard against her chin, but Mab didn't care. Because he was there, and he was alive, and she was going to make sure he stayed that way.

"I'm thinking red for your new wardrobe," she teased, gently helping him step into the tub. "We can go shopping when you're feeling up to it. I'll even let you snap us all over Milan if that's what you want."

"Okay," Ander said, the word more a sigh than anything else, and he nodded. "Okay."

They'd get back to normal eventually, Mab was sure of it. But for the time being, she was content to provide him with assurance and comfort and whatever else he might need. That's what family did.

Chapter 19
Ander

Helicon, Underworld - September 1862

Warm sun filtered in through the floor-to-ceiling windows, dancing over his skin in a reverent manner. From one of the partially open windows, the fluid strains of a harp filtered in, bringing a sense of peace to the early morning.

The tranquility of the moment was not lost on Ander. It had been many months since he had felt this safe, this calm.

It hadn't been all wonders and contentment since he'd returned home with Mab and his mother a week ago. Each night, he woke from a nightmare: Enrique coming to take him back, Ikari's battered body falling limp to the floor, Hades demanding that he stay with Enrique forever.

But each time he had woken, Mab had been there to hold him. Soothing him with her gentle words and comforting arms. He didn't have to wonder what he would do without her because each time he opened his eyes, there she was. Just as she had promised.

Rolling over, Ander found Mab facing him in the bed, the covers tucked up under her chin. Her white curls were bound in a silk scarf to keep them from frizzing out of control, and her dark lashes rested against her cheeks. Ander's lips twitched with an effortless smile, his first in a long time.

For so long, Ander had thought the only person in the world who loved him was his mother. It had made him accept the incomplete and inadequate love that others gave him, no matter what form it was offered in. But here was Mab, who had showed up in his life unexpectedly, and she loved him. Truly and deeply. In an unconditional way that asked for nothing from him but that he love her in return.

She was his best friend. His family. And he had known deep down that if he sent word to her, she would come for him.

"Stop staring," she grumbled, tucking herself further into the bedding.

"Never."

"Why?" Mab whined and peeked one eye open at him.

"Because, my dearest Mabbers, you're the most beautiful thing I've seen in months!"

She smacked him lightly in the face, and he couldn't help but laugh. The sound startled him, seeming foreign and a little broken. But it was true and heartfelt. Reaching out, Ander slipped his arms around her warm body and pulled her in against his chest, tucking her head beneath his chin. A sigh released from him that carried with it the weight of sorrows finally able to be let go.

They lay there for a while, just content in each other's embrace. So long that Ander wondered if Mab had fallen back to sleep.

"I'm sorry that I didn't listen to you when you said Enrique was bad news and was only going to hurt me." The words were whispered, and he waited, his heart beating rapidly in his chest, to see if she would respond.

"Oh, Andy, no. It's okay."

"No, it's not. You were only trying to protect me, and instead of listening to you, I let myself get swept away on the promise of false love. Like always."

Mab was silent for a moment, and Ander could feel the resistance in her body. She wanted to argue with him but was holding herself back. Instead, she said, "If there's ever a next time, I won't let you leave."

Ander gave her a squeeze and kissed the top of her head. "You're the best little sister a mongrel like me could ever ask for," he muttered.

"Same to you."

"I'm the best sister?" Ander's lips twitched.

"Yep."

Ander laughed again, and some of the pain and sorrow inside of him began to thaw out. There was still so much of it, he wasn't sure when he would feel normal again. But here in Helicon, with the love and support of his mother and Mab, Ander knew healing would happen.

Perhaps this time, he would be able to pay more attention to the love of those who deserved it and less to the ones who didn't.

"Want to get entirely too drunk?"

"Sure," Mab muttered into his chest. "Why not."

They drank all day, and then when the evening meal came around, they simply carried on drinking. Ander found himself unable to choke down even a little of the delicious looking meal but was quite happy to refill his goblet each time it was emptied.

It wasn't the dizzy spins that kept him drinking but the way he and Mab had fallen back into their old, ridiculous behavior. There wasn't any flirting with strangers, or having sex in hall closets with married men, but there was laughter, dancing. Childish games and loud, unsophisticated singing of whatever bawdy shanty crossed their minds. In the end, Queen Aemiliana told them that if they couldn't contain themselves enough at the table to behave like adults, they could retire to Ander's nursery for the night. But there was a light in her eye that spoke of happiness and relief.

Calling for more wine to be brought to his rooms, Ander and Mab walked arm in arm, teetering back and forth down the hallway.

Back in his suite, they flopped down on some of the' chaises in front of the fireplace and laughed breathlessly. Ander was so tipsy, he wasn't even sure anymore what they were laughing over, but it didn't seem to matter. The levity, and the ability to feel it without needing to censor himself, was so relieving.

"Do you know what I keep thinking about?" He slurred a little.

"That you're a pretty, pretty sister?" Mab snickered, finding herself incredibly funny.

Ander waved his hand at her. "No, that I'm terrible at choosing love." Mab sobered up a little, her brow pinching, so he continued before she could say anything. "I shouldn't be allowed to choose. I should take the choosing out of the equation."

"Andy . . ."

"No, listen!" Ander slid off his chaise lounge onto the floor like a wet towel slipping off the side of a table. Then he fell forward onto his hands and knees so that he could crawl across the floor until he reached Mab. Resting his head on her knee, he peered up at her, making his eyes as wide and becoming as he could. "Let's cast a spell."

"Um . . . sounds like a terrible idea."

"Come now, Mab! Don't be like that. It'll be great fun!"

"No."

"Yes! It'll be a love spell to Venus, asking her to send my soulmate to me. It's a brilliant idea!" he insisted.

"Andy—"

"No more of that." He brushed her off, reaching up to cover her lips with his fingers. Losing his balance, he toppled over onto the floor.

"You can't even sit up right now. How can you do a spell? What if you take your eyebrows off?" This sent her into a fit of snickers.

"Silence, banshee." Ander pressed a hand over his eyes. "I just need the room to stop spinning."

Once the room had settled down, Ander climbed carefully to his feet. Bustling around the room, he gathered what ingredients he had out of his cabinet and returned to the seating area. Dumping everything onto the floor, he eyed the room.

"Help me move these out of the way!" he demanded, kicking out at the chaise nearest to him.

Grunting her protest, Mab stood and began helping to push the furniture back so they were left with a nice, empty space. Once they had the room, Ander sprinkled sand onto the floor in a large circle.

"Help me set out these candles."

"Do you even know what you're doing?"

Ander gasped. "Of course I do."

When they were finished, candles and rose petals sat all

around the sand circle. In its center, a large gold urn awaited him. Stepping into the circle, Ander beckoned Mab in with him.

"No, I'm good out here. I don't need a love spell."

"Come on, I just need you here for reassurance and encouragement."

Mab sighed irritably but stepped into the circle.

Once they were seated across from each other with their legs folded beneath them, Ander wove his hands over the urn, igniting a pink flame. Picking up the dried myrtle beside him, he rubbed it between his hands, crumpling it up.

"Oh, Venus, beautiful life-giving goddess of love, I ask for your help." Ander sprinkled the myrtle over the pink flame. "Using your wisdom concerning the heart, find me my soulmate. Send them to me and let no one else claim my heart until they appear."

Once the last of the myrtle was in the fire, Ander extended both his hands to Mab.

"What?"

"Give me your hands."

"Why?"

"Maaaaab." Ander sighed her name roughly, eyeing her. Rolling her own eyes, she finally slapped her hands into his. "Now, close your eyes and think of me finding the perfect lover."

"I think you mean love."

"I think I mean both." Ander grinned, then shut his eyes. Calling his magic to him, he muttered under his breath, tying the spell up into a beautiful package before he sent it out into the world in a puff of bright pink smoke, the scent of roses mingling with myrtle.

Silence filled the room when it was done, and both

Ander and Mab slowly opened their eyes to stare over at each other.

"Now what?" Mab asked.

"Well . . . now I guess we wait."

"And drink?"

"Oh, and most certainly drink."

Epilogue
Ander

Berlin, Germany - July 1995

Around them, the music blasted, the beat hitting his chest with such rapid force that Ander felt like he was vibrating. Around his neck he wore a glow stick necklace, and several matching bracelets ran down his bare arms. His lean but muscular body was clad in a pair of low-hung blue camouflage cargo pants and a white mesh tank top.

His hair, which he had dyed red with black tips, was spiked up all over his head. His lidded, dark brown eyes were outlined in smudged black, and his nails painted black to match.

He danced freely and wholeheartedly, letting the music sweep him away.

Mab, jumping up and down to the beat of the music beside him, was dressed almost identically, except her camouflage pants were gray, her tank top was solid, and her curls were streaked with pink highlights he'd forced on her.

They had been dancing for what seemed like hours

when Mab leaned in to shout into his ear. "I'm too hot, can we grab a breather outside?"

Nodding, Ander grabbed her hand and tugged her through the crush of people. Once they were outside of the warehouse, Ander leaned up against the building, breathing in the night air. In the wee hours of the morning, it was a little cool, and it felt nice on his feverish skin.

"This DJ is not the best I've ever listened to. But he gets the job done, I suppose." Reaching into his pocket, Ander pulled out his little tin of cigarettes. Opening the canister, he plucked one from inside and set it between his lips. He lit it with the tip of his finger and breathed in the smoke, slowly blowing it back out his nose.

"Those are so gross," Mab muttered, lifting her hair up off the back of her neck. She then reached out to pluck the cigarette from his lips and took a puff.

"Of course I would find the two of you outside a disreputable establishment such as this."

Both Ander and Mab turned toward the voice to find Erotes standing before them. A nervous laugh slipped from Ander's lips. He had managed to avoid the god of love for 130 years, sneaking out before he was spotted any time they wound up at the same parties or events. Yet, here he was, on a random street in Berlin, looking incredibly pleased with himself.

"Erotes . . . what a surprise and pleasure." Ander shot Mab a look. Though she hadn't been there the night Erotes had chased Ander outside in front of some mortals, she had heard all about it. Mab was looking back at him, eyebrows high on her face. "I didn't realize you were a fan of the German rave scene—"

"Enough of your idle chatter," he cut him off. "Do you

know what this is, Ander Ruin?" Erotes held up a sheet of paper.

Squinting at it, Ander stole his cigarette back and took a long drag. "A license to wear that god awful suit?" His eyes fell to take in the cream slacks and blazer that looked like they had come straight out of *Miami Vice*.

Erotes glared at him, and Mab coughed lightly in warning—or laughter—it was honestly hard to tell with her sometimes.

"This is the spell you cast to my mother over a hundred years ago, requesting a soulmate be found for you. Tragically, it was misplaced for all this time, but now that it's been uncovered . . ." The slow smile that spread over Erotes' face made Ander's skin turn ice-cold. "I've come to fulfill your request."

"That's really not necessary . . ." Ander had forgotten he'd ever cast that spell, it had been so long ago. Now, however, that drunken night came rushing back.

"Oh, but it really is. After all, shame on both Mother and I for having misplaced your request for so long."

Ander held up his hand to beg for mercy when Erotes replaced the paper with his gold bow and a glowing arrow. Ander wouldn't have thought anything of it, but he could feel the way the arrow tugged at him, making him want to follow it.

"What are you . . . going to do with that?" He tried to sound casual, but there was sweat forming at his temples, and his voice came out a little forced.

As if the world decided to respond instead, a rumble rippled through the air, and a thunderstorm came up from what seemed like a previously cloudless sky. The clouds were purple and blue, something fiery brewing in their depths. Ander recognized the storm for what it was: Prometheus delivering the next batch of ignis to the earth.

His eyes dropped to Erotes, dread starting at his toes and working its way up. "Erotes, let's talk. I apologize for your wife, really. But she was the one who came on to me, I was simply too weak at the time to refuse—"

Erotes aimed toward the thunderstorm, and as a bright light shot down from the clouds, he fired the arrow directly into the bolt.

"*Oh, come on!*" The shout slipped out of him, unbidden and uncontrollable. "An ignis? *Really?!*"

Erotes was grinning once again, a dark, vengeful look in his eyes. "Did you know Prometheus is said to have made them incapable of falling in love at Indra's behest? He didn't want anything getting in the way of their mission."

"You . . . You *asshole*! I'll have you know, if I ever meet your wife again, I'll make her forget your name altogether!"

"Ander . . ." Mab grunted, smacking him on the hip. "You're only going to make it worse for yourself." Her words were from the corner of her lips as she attempted to look as chill as she possibly could.

"No, he's being a dick, Mab. He just shot my arrow at a damn ignis out of *spite.*"

Erotes' eyes had narrowed on him. "You would further insult me?"

"Yes, I would damn well further insult you! That was supposed to be my *one* chance!"

Erotes pulled out another arrow.

"What are you doing?" Ander asked him. Beside him, Mab's hand lifted unconsciously to her chest as she felt the pull of the arrow.

"If you won't learn your lesson for yourself, perhaps you will learn it for your friend." The next flash of lightning came, and Erotes' new arrow followed, directly into the bolt. Same as before, but now it was Mab who took an involuntary step forward as if tugged by a string.

"No!" Mab squawked, realization dawning on her. Before Ander could say anything else, her hand was clamping over his mouth, and she was pinning him to the wall. "Shut up. Just shut *up!*"

Growling against her fingers, and then licking them so she'd quickly pull her hand back, Ander glowered at Erotes.

"Enjoy your soulmates," the god of love called over his shoulder as he walked away, disappearing down an alley.

"What did you *do?*" Mab shouted. "Ander, what did you just *do?!*"

"I didn't do anything!" he snapped back.

But Erotes had.

He'd done something incredibly petty.

Out there, somewhere, two infant ignis were falling to the earth to be found by their future Guardians. And if they managed to make it to adulthood without dying or being captured by the enemy . . . they would be bound to Ander and Mab for all eternity—whether they could fall in love or not.

Sneak Peek!

continue reading for a sneak peek of Sanctuary of the Lost
Book 1: Of Love & Ruin

LOU WILHAM & CHRISTIS CHRISTIE

Prologue
Ander

Miami, Florida – September 2005

It was hotter than the pits of Acheron today, but the satisfaction of what was about to come helped to cool Ander like nothing else could.

Today, Ezequiel 'Zeke' Schields would get his due.

Exactly two years ago, Ander and Mab had moved to Miami following Ander's bright idea to open a world-class nightclub, catering to mortals and Underworlders alike. The location had been easy enough to settle on, the design already pictured perfectly in Ander's mind, and even the name had come to him without hesitation: Inferno. The one issue that had made itself prevalent on opening day—and every day since—had been Zeke Schields, the owner of the nightclub across the street.

Eighteen months after signing the papers for the new location, Inferno had opened to a long line of excited Underworld residents and humans all clambering to get in. When Zeke had shown up and introduced himself, Ander thought he had come to welcome them to the neighborhood and perhaps offer a word of congratulations. Instead, he had informed Ander that Inferno was little better than a trashy pimp's showroom, and they would be out of business in two weeks.

Mab had barely been able to restrain Ander from lighting Zeke's clothes on fire and dancing around his flaming body. He'd had to settle instead for the notion of taking the other nightclub down by whatever means necessary.

Six months later, the two nightclubs were both still going strong but took every opportunity to undermine each other.

"You really didn't need to come," Mitchell, the health inspector, said for the second time since Ander had met him outside Element 79. He was badly balding, with sweat stains forming on his short-sleeved dress shirt and a tie that was clearly clipped on.

"No, I most certainly needed to be here." Ander wasn't missing this moment for anything. After all, he had to be certain that they *found* the rats he had magically planted inside the club last week.

Ander tugged at the collar of his wine-colored velvet Louis Vuitton blazer. On top of a white V-neck T-shirt and black skinny jeans, the blazer was definitely too much, and he was sweating profusely. Fortunately, unlike Mitchell-the-health-inspector, his sweating was not noticeable, and a small snap of his fingers magicked it away for the second time since he had arrived.

To top the look off, he had added glitter dust to his horns and adorned his fingers in a number of gold rings and bands. He felt fierce, and it bolstered his confidence.

Beneath the blistering sun, a white taxi van pulled up along the sidewalk. When the side door slid violently open, a little boy and a little girl launched themselves out wearing harnesses—which they were *much* too old for—attached to leashes that were in the hands of Zeke Schields. He climbed out over the two kids, who were now fighting. The little girl pinned the boy to the ground only for him to flip her and tangle the leashes even more.

On Zeke's back was a carrier from which a toddler flailed her limbs, crying most unhappily at being contained in the oversized Baby Bjorn. Squinting at her, Ander realized there were a pair of pink wings—like they'd been ripped off of a flamingo—also flapping rapidly on her back.

The last to emerge from the van was a young boy, likely around nine or ten, who seemed to be the only Schields somewhat in control of himself at the moment. He was dressed in a light blue polo shirt and dark navy button-up cardigan. Ander would have been shocked at the sight of the sweater if it weren't for the pair of brilliantly white wings gracing his back.

Ignis—notoriously known for being fans of heat and also, apparently, Zeke's oldest and youngest children.

Frack! Zeke Schields was a Guardian.

It didn't change anything. *Couldn't* change anything. Ander wouldn't back down. No matter Schields' connection to the Sanctum.

The eldest wiggled an open candy bar in front of the toddler, calming her wailing for the moment, while Zeke attempted to untangle the two leashes, separating the middle children with his foot.

"Behave, you beasts!" Zeke grumbled at them, then eyed the health inspector with irritation. "Let's get this over with."

Schields handed the leash attached to the little girl over to his eldest child and then dug a set of keys out of his very tight jeans. Stepping up to the front door to unlock it, he sent Ander a scathing look.

"This was you, wasn't it?" he hissed at him, shoving the door open dramatically. Ander merely shrugged and waved a hand before him to indicate he was uncertain what was going on. Schields only glared further, then turned back to the oldest. "Stay out here with your sister, I can't do this with both the twins inside."

Schields and Mitchell-the-health-inspector disappeared into the club, leaving Ander and the two children outside.

Leaning against the hot brick wall, Ander gazed down at the boy holding the leash of his little sister, who was struggling against the restraint, attempting to get away with soft grunts of effort. "Le'go!" she growled.

The boy—clearly using his baby-ignis strength to help him—appeared to be holding her back with little effort.

"Cute pet you've got there," Ander said, not really certain what to do as he waited.

The boy frowned. "This is my sister." His tone held offense.

Ander smirked. "Are you sure? I have a puppy I don't even treat this much like an animal." He nodded at the little girl, who'd accepted her defeat and was currently pulling a Lilo, lying facedown on the sidewalk. "I think she's asking to be left to die."

Several emotions drifted over the boy's face, and Ander wondered what series of thoughts were drifting through his mind. Finally, he settled on asking, "You have a puppy? What kind?"

Ander blinked at the change in subject. "A teacup Pomeranian."

"What's its name?"

"*Her* name is Princess Monaco—Monnie, for short."

The small ignis grinned suddenly. "She's a princess."

"Yes, she is." And how so. He'd only brought her home a little over a month ago, and already she ruled the roost. Mab was continually at him for his overindulgence of the animal. But he simply couldn't help himself.

The boy's smile faltered as his brows screwed up and another thought clearly came to him. "What did my papa mean by 'this was you'?" His bright hazel eyes, which bore a look of concern, shifted toward the door through which his father and the inspector had disappeared, then returned to focus on Ander. Dark strands of his fluffy hair fell into his eyes, but that didn't seem to impede him. "Did you do something?"

Beneath the steady, inquisitive gaze of the young ignis, Ander nearly squirmed. "And if I did?" He felt haughty, saucy—defensive.

"Then that was very bad of you." His brow creased more, a look of near disappointment crossing his features. Though he was young, the soldier was there beneath the surface, just waiting to emerge. The vanquisher of all social injustices.

"Maybe. Maybe not. Maybe it was warranted and deserved."

The boy was still frowning. "He's very stressed, you know. Daddy left for Syria last week, and we don't know when he'll be back. Papa has a hard time with the twins and Georgie all by himself."

He was eyeing Ander as if all of this were his doing and he'd heaped the stress down upon them. "Well, as unfortunate as that may all be, I have no control over whether your *Papa* is a good father or not."

The boy clearly took offense to this. "He's a good papa!"

Ander lifted his hands up. "My apologies." Though,

from what he'd seen, Zeke Schields was in way over his head with four children. Two of whom were ignis, which meant a great amount of training and preparation for their future duties.

The life of a Guardian was a rigorous and difficult one. The Sanctum, from what Ander understood, expected a lot out of the couples raising their future soldiers to adulthood.

"Are you the one who owns the . . . the whore house across the street?"

Ander glared. "Nightclub," he corrected. "There may be whores but no buying or selling. And yes, I am."

"Papa says you're his arch nemesis. I'm not really sure what that means, except that he has to *end you*."

Ander could only smirk in delight. "So he talks about me, then."

Clearly, he had gotten under Schields' skin. That pleased him greatly.

The boy huffed and looked down at his sister, who was now poking at a bug crawling across the sidewalk in front of her, muttering her grievances to it. He must have decided she was fairly harmless at the moment, for his eyes drifted back up to Ander.

Or rather, Ander's head.

He squinted, then his face relaxed a little. "You have sparkly horns . . ." His eyes then fell to Ander's feet and shoes. "But no hooves." He met his eyes next. "What kind of Underworlder are you?"

Wouldn't he like to know? Wouldn't *Ander* like to know? "Some say I'm the devil."

He shook his head. "No, you're not the devil. You're too pretty." The little ignis blushed, a charming shade that made his hazel eyes sparkle.

Ander chuckled, amused at the kid's reaction. "Too pretty to be the devil? What if that's the point?"

The boy shook his head. "No, there is no devil in Underworld. Just Hades, who the humans don't believe in anymore."

Oh, there were plenty of devils in Underworld. It simply depended on your definition of evil.

"I am half muse. The other half, no one knows for sure."

"Muse . . ." He fell silent then and looked to be in deep thought. "The muses live in . . . in . . . Heel . . . Heel—"

"Helicon. Yes. That is where I am from."

He nodded. "And do all muses have pretty horns?"

Ander chuckled again and shook his head. "No, I am the only muse with horns. That's why they all think perhaps my father was a satyr."

"Oh. But satyrs are the servant race. Right?"

He was a smart kid, it would seem. Schields had taught him well. Or maybe it was his partner, this unnamed 'Daddy', who was responsible for all the schooling.

"Yes, they are."

"Oh."

"Mmm." Ander's eyes fell to the girl. "Your sister is eating that bug."

"Nox! NO!" The boy dropped down to fish his fingers into the girl's mouth. She began screeching, kicking, and hitting at this invasion.

It was at this moment that Schields and the inspector stepped outside. Schields looked harried and upset, dark fury in his eyes as they landed on Ander. "I hope you're happy," he snarled. "I've been shut down for two weeks due to a *rodent* infestation." He handed the leash of the little boy to the eldest and then stooped to pick up the screeching little girl. "Is that a bug leg on your lip?!" He gasped in horror, plucking it from her mouth. "Seriously, you're seven years old. Whyyyy?"

Ander watched the scene, dead-positive he would never subject himself to the horror of having children.

Behind them, the inspector was stapling a notice to the door that said the facility was closed until approval from the health board had been issued.

"It's a tragedy, really," Ander said, a smirk hitting the corner of his lips.

Schields whipped his head around to stare him down. "Don't think for one moment that I don't know you're behind this and that I won't find a way to destroy you. This will not be the end of me, Ruin."

"It's in the name, darling: ruin. It's what I do best." Ask any life he'd touched in his three hundred years on Earth. Destruction and ruin were what followed in his wake. Even when he meant only the best.

Schields glared and then turned to say goodbye to the inspector. "Come, you hooligans, we're going home." The youngest boy cheered and darted for the street, just barely stopped by his older brother from careening out in front of a cab that was pulling up in front of the club.

Ander couldn't help himself as he watched Schields attempting to herd his children like a pack of wild cats into the taxi. "Schields, don't think of this as a loss for the club. Instead, think of it as a boon for your family. A chance to learn how to handle fatherhood."

Schields froze, his shoulders stiffening. Instead of responding, he just finished getting the smaller children into the van before climbing in himself.

The eldest, who Ander had been conversing with, did turn though. There was a look of devastation and deep disappointment on his face. Slowly, he shook his head at Ander.

Ander didn't expect it, but he felt a wash of shame rising up inside him.

Before he could apologize, Schields reached out of the van to grab the boy's arm and pull him up into the vehicle.

Just as the door was shutting, with one last view of bright white wings, Ander felt a twang of something deep and pulling in his chest. Gasping, he raised his fingers to rub at the space right over his heart.

"Oh . . . fuck." Not waiting to watch the cab drive away, Ander darted across the street without even looking and hurled himself through the front doors of Inferno. "Mab!" he shouted frantically. "*Mab!*" He screeched her name this time.

"What?!" Mab growled, stepping out of the back storage room behind the fine Brazilian cherrywood bar.

"We have to leave. Right now. Right *now*."

"What? Leave for where? I have to prep; we open in a few hours."

Ander raced over to her, slapping his hands down on the surface of the bar that had cost him thousands of dollars to buy, ship, and have installed. "Forget that. We're leaving Miami. I can't stay here."

Mab frowned in confusion. "What the hell do you mean? Ander, we just got our liquor license six months ago. Inferno is doing great. We're not leaving."

"But I think I've found him. *He's here in this city.*"

"Ander. Words that make sense, for the love of the gods, please."

"Erotes. The arrow. Ignis." He was panting, trying to catch his breath as anxiety filled him. "I think I just met my soulmate."

Mab chuckled darkly. "I don't care."

Ander blinked. "What?"

"You heard me. I don't care. We're not leaving."

"But."

"No." With that, Mab turned and walked back into the storage room. Her last word on the matter was the rattling of wine bottles as she worked on stocking for that night's opening.

Acknowledgments

Of Loyalties & Wreckage was a passion project for us. Mab and Ander are characters we created years ago on a RPG site, and never in our wildest dreams did we think they'd ever see the light of day. When we first began discussing the notion of co-authoring something together, there was never any question about what story we should do. The characters were there already, begging to be let out into the world. For this reason, we want to say a big thank you to everyone who stumbled upon this novella and decided to give Mab and Ander a chance. We hope their story speaks to you, just like it continues to speak to us.

There is something special about the found family a person chooses to surround themselves with, and we would be nothing without our fabulous family of fellow authors at Midnight Tide Publishing. Thank you all for your continued support through all aspects of the writing process! To our mutual bestie, Elle, thank you for being the push that got us both into this publishing game in the first place.

To our betas: Elle, Jordan, Candace, Jalessa, and Tanya you are all amazing! Your comments and insights helped Of Loyalties & Wreckage become the book it is today and we can't thank you enough.

Meg. Oh, Meg. We have nothing but praise for our grammar queen! (And we write ALL the suspicion just for you) You never bemoan our comma use, be it excessive or lacking, and you help make each sentence shine. Thank you.

Lastly, we want to thank the friends who support, encourage and maintain. Life is nothing without our besties, and it's because of them that we laugh, boast more confidence than we have on our own, and sometimes make truly terrible (but also amazing) decisions.

Give your bestie a tight hug for us!
     XO

About Christis Christie

 Christis Christie was born and raised in a small town in New Brunswick, Canada where she spent most of her time either reading someone else's book, or dreaming of writing her own. Her favourite thing to dive into is an epic fantasy, or anything else magical and wondrous that really allows her imagination to take her away.

She now lives on the East Coast in Halifax, Nova Scotia where she works as an event designer, putting her interior decorating degree to wonderful use. Whenever she's not busy magically transforming venues for her clients, Christis is working on her own writing.

Her other dreams consist of one day visiting Ireland so she can frolic over the hills, and owning a teacup Pomeranian she can cart around everywhere with her.

Also By Christis Christie

Spun Gold: A Rumpelstiltskin Origin Story

Reaping Book One: Epheus

Sanctuary of the Lost
    Of Loyalties and Wreckage

Anthologies
    Cirque de vol Mystique
    Something in the Shadows: A Halloween Anthology
    Emporium of Superstition - An Old Wives' Tale Anthology

Co-Authored with Elle Beaumont:
    The Dragon's Bride
    Seeds of Sorrow (Immortal Realms Book 1)

About Lou Wilham

Born and raised in a small town near the Chesapeake Bay, Lou Wilham grew up on a steady diet of fiction, arts and crafts, and Old Bay. After years of absorbing everything, there was to absorb of fiction, fantasy, and sci-fi she's left with a serious writing/drawing habit that just won't quit. These days, she spends much of her time writing, drawing, and chasing a very short Basset Hound named Sherlock.

When not, daydreaming up new characters to write and draw she can be found crocheting, making cute bookmarks, and binge-watching whatever happens to catch her eye.

Learn more about Lou and her future projects on her website: http://louinprogress.com/ or join her mailing list at: http://subscribepage.com/mailermailer

facebook.com/LouWilham

instagram.com/lou.wilham

Also By Lou Wilham

The Curse Collection
 The Curse of The Black Cat
 The Curse of Ash and Blood
 The Curse of Flour and Feeling

The Clockwork Chronicles
 The Girl in the Clockwork Tower
 The Unicorn and the Clockwork Quest
 The Rose in the Clockwork Library

The Heir To Moondust
 The Prince of Starlight
 The Prince of Daybreak

The Witches of Moondale
 The Hex Next Door

Sanctuary of the Lost
 Of Loyalties and Wreckage

Completed Series
The Tales of the Sea Trilogy
Villainous Heroics

More Books You'll Love

If you enjoyed this story, please consider leaving a review.

Then check out more books from Midnight Tide Publishing!

The Devil You Know by Nicole Northwood

In the Underworld, nothing ever changes.

When the demon of Lust, Cam, decides he needs an overhaul in his 'life after death', he leaves the Second Circle of Hell to run an indulgent hotel and club in the heart of New York City. As his lover, Lucifer, bides his time to create a bargain to have Cam return, Cam is permitted to explore the human world, but not without being led into temptation. A group of demon hunters disguised as police set out to send Cam back into the fires of Hell by getting him lost in desire for one of their own, but things very quickly take an unexpected turn—Cam's fallen in love with the Hedonism Hotel's night manager, Giselle, and he won't leave Earth so easily.

Within the liminal space of hotels and their surroundings, paranormal beings and the humans who love them travel together on intimate journeys of self discovery while learning to trust one another with the things that make them unique. Each of the seven stories in the Hotel Heat series takes the reader through a steamy romance with new main characters while featuring fan-favorite major and minor characters who have appeared in earlier novels, and will continue to appear in upcoming books.

Available Now

Syren's Mutiny by Jessica S. Taylor

"It's frightful bad luck to have a woman aboard."

Brigid knew the superstition, but when her father tried to marry her off, she had no choice but to stowaway on a ship bound for Bhodheas. When she's discovered and discarded, her fate seems sealed...until she's saved by the ocean and its queen.

Transformed into a syren and given new life, Brigid now has the power to seek revenge on those who wronged her.

Caelum has spent his entire life trying to help those who couldn't help themselves. After years suffering the cruelty of his pirate father, saving others from a similar fate was ingrained in him. But when he's unable to save a young girl from being thrown overboard for hiding away, he's devastated.

Until one day, when he's thrown into the water by unforeseen forces, he comes face to face with the past, and maybe, with his future.

But there's a darkness lurking on the seas they both call home. And Caelum and Brigid have no idea just how intertwined their stories really are.

Available Now

Her Dark Reflection by Hailey Jade

"They called me the Whore Queen. Some even called me the Evil Queen.

But they could call me whatever they wanted. I was still queen."

Rhiandra Tiercelin hungers for power and her charm has always been her sharpest weapon in hunting it. So when a brutal attack leaves her physically scarred, desperation drives her to make a deal with Draven, a magic-wielding stranger who is inexplicably compelling and definitely dangerous. She knows she can't trust him, but when he offers to make her a queen, the temptation is too enticing to resist.

Armed with a glamoured face and an enchanted apple, Rhiandra is determined to scheme her way into a crown, even if it means risking the deadly punishment for unsanctioned magic use. But Draven is playing a bigger game, and she is just one piece on the board.

Can she keep her wits about her long enough to uncover his secrets, or will he lure her down a path she will come to regret?

Her Dark Reflection is the first book in a new dark fantasy series perfect for fans of Raven Kennedy, Jennifer Armentrout and Sarah A. Parker. If you like cunning, ambitious heroines, morally ambiguous men and slow burn romance that toes the line between love and hate, then you'll love Hailey Jade's dark reimagining of Snow White and the Seven Dwarves.

Available Now